Charlie Crow
and
The Vanishing River

With best wishes,
Jean Kelly.

JEAN KELLY

Illustrated by Emma Colbert

Postcrow
Press

First published 2013
by Postcrow Press
www.postcrow.com
www.facebook.com/fizzlemefeathers

© Jean Kelly (text and characters)
© Emma Colbert (illustrations)

ISBN: 978-0-9926570-0-0
Printed by Rosehill Press

Design and typesetting by Alan Steenson

For family and friends everywhere

Contents

Parkanaur Forest

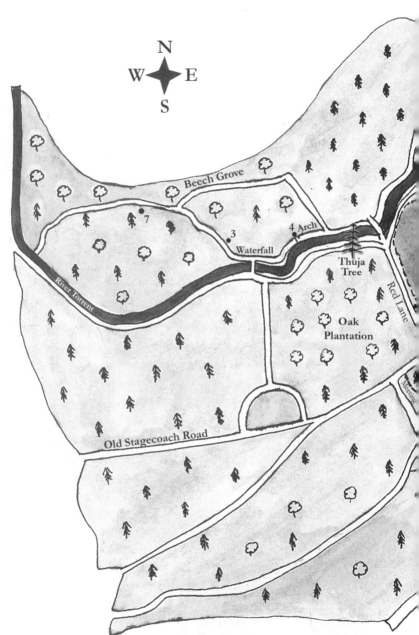

Our Homes

1. **Oak Drey**
   Norman and Lily Grey Squirrel

2. **Sandy Warren**
   Joseph and Madge Rabbit

3. **Denvale Earth**
   Alexander Fox

4. **Nest - in - the - Burrow**
   Mavis Wood Mouse

5. **Honeysuckle Nest**
   Marie-Claire and Percy Hedgehog

6. **Rush Lair**
   Owen, Maria and Lucy Fallow Deer

7. **Bridge Hill Sett**
   Patrick and Jenny Badger

8. **Rory's Nest**
   Rory Robin

Parkanaur Forest

As you enter through the faded, black railings and pass the deserted gate lodge, you know this is no ordinary forest. Over the small, stone bridge and up the hill takes you to the Big House, still impressive but with a formal garden sad from neglect.

Hundreds of years ago it was the people who lived in the Big House who ordered their workers to plant the trees. Thousands of trees and saplings were planted by men using spades. The men are long gone but everywhere giant oak, ash and beech trees reach to the sky, the legacy of their efforts.

You can follow the old stagecoach route that runs through the Deer Park but be sure to close the gates behind you. If you turn right at the far end of the Deer Park and walk down the Red Lane watch out for the ghost of a headless horseman. He is not the only strange sight you might see in this forest. For those willing to explore, Parkanaur is full of magical places, some only known to those who live here. Make no mistake, if you enter this forest today you will be watched by those who now call it home – although you may not see them.

Some Inhabitants of Parkanaur

Charlie Crow knows everyone in the forest and their business! He's a confident crow. He's a likeable chap whom everyone trusts.

Rory Robin speaks his mind and doesn't care if he offends anyone. He is a cheeky bird who enjoys an argument and is afraid of no-one. He considers himself to be something of a "cool dude".

Bert Kingfisher likes to think others see him as a sharp dresser and creative thinker. He tries to portray himself as strong and confident but actually he is quite shy and insecure.

Seamus Grey Heron is a sincere and gentle soul who thinks the world of his wife, Marjorie, whom he is very protective towards.

Marjorie Grey Heron respects her husband but is her own heron, capable, confident and courageous.

Malachy Mallard is a duck who generally keeps himself to himself although he is always willing to help others when they are in need. Occasionally, he can become a little over-excited and flustered.

Winston Crow can be rather pompous but is good in a crisis and commands the respect of his fellow rooks. He has excellent organisational skills.

Barney Crow loves to be the centre of attention. He's all talk and no action. Barney is more concerned for himself than others and when the going gets tough, Barney beats a hasty retreat!

Norman Grey Squirrel is a total grump who permanently feels hard done by. He's married to Lily who is kind and long suffering. She always tries to see the good in her fellow creatures.

Terry Red Squirrel is a squirrel with a sense of purpose and is not easily intimidated. He cares deeply about his family, as does his wife, Teresa, who is more easily frightened and for whom friendship is very important.

Mavis Wood Mouse is an excellent cook and very hospitable although rather prone to the giggles.

Charlie Crow
and
The Vanishing River

1

Rain but no Water!

Flippity flap, flippity flap, gosh but my wings are heavy this morning. The rain hasn't stopped all night and I can tell you it's a jolly good thing my postbag is waterproof. I've a letter for Bert Kingfisher but I tried his nest at the pond and he's not there.

My name's Charlie, by the way, Charlie Crow. My Mother was a rather attractive rook, that's a member of the crow family for those of you who aren't too sure of your birds. My Father was the postcrow in this forest before I took over. I collect and deliver the letters to all the forest residents, well the furred and feathered variety at least. The humans who live in the Big House have their own arrangements.

Malachy Mallard suggested I try the waterfall as Bert Kingfisher often perches there so that's where I'm headed now. I'll follow the river upstream to get there, that's quickest. It's strange with all this rain that the river's not higher. Oops, cornering the bend after the Dry Stone Arch, underneath the Deodar Cedar, is always a bit tricky. So sad that the Deodar was broken in the great storm, it used to be so magnificent, one of my absolute favourite trees in the forest, it and the Tulip tree.

There's Bert. He's so tiny but unmistakeable in his orange and blue feathers. He's perching on a branch overhanging the waterfall. The water is only trickling over the stones below him and Bert's looking rather forlorn. As a crow, with rather boring, black and bedraggled feathers, it's a bit difficult to feel sorry for my flashy-feathered, kingfisher friend. But he is my friend and I do feel sorry for him. With all the rain we had last night, the water should be gushing over the waterfall with plenty of fish for Bert's breakfast.

"Fizzle me feathers, Bert, I'm sure this is only temporary. The river's been this low before and the water always returns eventually." I can tell Bert needs to get something off his chest. I rest my postbag on the stone bridge as he points his long beak in my direction and begins a lecture on the selfishness of humans.

"They make me so cross, Charlie, they really do! Clearly humans have taken the water further upstream for their own purposes and it's just hard luck for the rest of us who need this river to survive. They don't care about us birds and animals. I mean, how are we supposed to find fish in this?"

Bert looks at the shallow covering of water running over the pebbly bottom of the river. I'm not sure how to respond. I'm curious though, what do humans do with all the water they take out of the rivers? Do they really need it all? They clearly aren't concerned about Bert and others who rely on the river for food. Talking of others, here come Marjorie and Seamus Grey Heron, wading upstream towards us. Seamus is frowning.

"Morning, Charlie. Morning, Bert. Well, this is a fine mess, isn't it? I was just saying to the missus what a mess this is. How's a grey heron supposed to find his breakfast in this excuse for a river? It's those humans at their work again, I'd bet my beak on it! How would they like it if we interfered with their world? Eh? Eh?"

Bert seizes on this idea.

"You might be on to something, Seamus. Maybe we could give those humans a taste of their own medicine and then they might think twice before upsetting our world!"

I know, I know, all humans are not nasty and selfish, but some are. For example, this business of diverting the water from our river has happened before. Bert seems to have decided that enough is enough.

"Seamus, why do the humans need to take our water? Have you any ideas?"

Seamus lowers his head and scratches it with his wing as he stands on one leg.

"Not a clue, Bert, simply not a clue." But it's obvious he's really not giving the matter much thought. Marjorie, on the other wing, seems to be taking Bert's question more seriously.

"I think most humans are really very kind. I don't know why they take our water but I'm sure they must have a very good reason for doing so." Well, at least humans have still got one friend in the forest, but I'm afraid Bert remains unimpressed. Marjorie is a very large bird and Bert is a very tiny bird, but this doesn't prevent him from launching a bitter attack on her.

"Marjorie Grey Heron, are you a complete twit? How can you stand there with barely a foot covered with water, in a river that should be at least up to your knees, and tell us that humans must have a very good reason for taking our water! Do you really think that they would go hungry if they hadn't taken our water? We're certainly going hungry! Do you think they care? I don't think so."

Poor Marjorie, despite the fact that she could easily knock Bert off his perch with one flick of her wing, looks quite chastened.

"Well, it's just that I often see the humans bringing bread to the park to feed us birds and I always thought that it was such a kind thing to do."

Bert's beak shakes with rage and he positively quivers as he screams at the startled Marjorie,

"Oh yes, very kind. They bring us some mouldy, old bread that they wouldn't eat themselves, whilst at the same time stealing our lovely, fresh fish by taking our river water, oh yes, very kind indeed."

I feel I should say that Bert is not usually this angry but hunger can have that effect. He is, of course, assuming that all humans are the same. All crows are not the same, nor are all kingfishers, so I don't suppose all humans are the same either. I believe that the humans who bring us the bread do so for kind reasons and, mouldy or not, I have to confess to enjoying their contributions. Sadly, they often chase us crows away in favour of Rory Robin and his mates. Still, we crows usually get some of the bread and we do enjoy it.

Marjorie Grey Heron and I may be looking for the good in the human race, but I'm afraid Bert seems more interested in teaching humans a lesson. In particular, he wants those who are responsible for taking the river water and, consequently, the fish from his river, to feel his wrath.

"I don't really care why they have taken our water," Bert continues a little more calmly, "but I think they need to be taught a lesson and that's just what I'm going to do."

Seamus Grey Heron is intrigued, as are we all.

"How are you going to do that then, Bert? Eh? Eh?"

"I'm not sure yet," replies Bert, "I'm going to devise a plan and I may need your help."

Seamus assures Bert that he will help in any way he can and he and Marjorie fly off. As I watch their slow, flapping wing beats lift them into the air, I pull out the letter I have for Bert. As he takes if from me, I ask him to keep me informed of his plan.

Eric Kingfisher's Letter

Nest-in the-Bank

Torrent's Turn

Dear Bert,

I really enjoyed that spot of fishing last Friday. I didn't expect to bump into you this far downstream but anytime you are flying past this way again do pop in, Jessica and I would both be delighted to see you.

Jessica has had a little trouble with her beak recently. She dived rather too enthusiastically and hit some sharp stones on the bottom of the river bed. Mind you, she got her fish, that's my Jess, never known to miss a fish yet!

We were actually thinking of organising some speed trials, would you be interested? Since all kingfishers are renowned for their speed we thought it might be fun to have a competition. Let me know if you or any of the other upstream kingfishers would be interested.

Best regards,

Eric.

Bert Kingfisher's Reply

Pond Bank Nest

Parkanaur Forest

Dear Eric,

How lovely to hear from you and Jessica. The speed trials sound like a lot of fun and believe me I could certainly be doing with some light relief at present.

The humans are taking our water again. They must be diverting it upstream and we are really worried as our fish supplies have been severely affected. I'm sure you must be having a similar problem by now. I really think it's time the humans were taught a lesson so I'm working on a plan, I'll let you know more about it when I have the details worked out.

Do send me some application forms for the speed trials and I'll try and find out if anyone else is interested. Is there an entrance fee? When exactly are you hoping to hold them?

I'll look forward to hearing from you soon.

Regards,

Bert.

2

New Residents

There's been a bit of bother in our forest recently. The grey squirrels were being trapped by the forest rangers. The grey squirrels damage the trees you see, but Lily Grey Squirrel, for example, is a lovely creature and so trapping *all* greys does seem a bit extreme. Then, as if to add insult to injury, some red squirrels wanted to return to Parkanaur Forest. Well, you should have heard Norman Grey Squirrel, that's Lily's husband, I do believe it was only his fear of being mistaken for a *red* that prevented him from exploding with rage!

In an effort to restore some harmony to our community we held a Big Meeting. It was agreed by all the animals here in Parkanaur Forest that a *small* number of red squirrels would be welcomed back. At the same time everyone also agreed that they would warn the grey squirrels if they spotted any traps. Last week Terry Red Squirrel, his wife, Teresa, and their family, all moved into the Deer Park. It was decided that the Deer Park, and *only* the Deer Park, would be home for any returning red squirrels. If this restriction had not been agreed then the grey squirrels might not have voted in favour of the reds' return.

Terry and Teresa Red Squirrel have built a very fine drey in one of the old lime trees. I'm just heading there now with yet more cards wishing them well in their new home. Well, I'm guessing that's what all this post is. Oh look, there's Terry tidying a few stray twigs on the drey.

"Caw, caw, caw! Hello, Terry, how are things? I've more post for you and Teresa today. You must have lots of friends!" Terry is a stocky squirrel and normally seems very confident but today he seems a bit down in the dumps and not a bit excited about receiving yet more post.

He looks me in the eye and asks,

"Charlie, are you glad to see us reds back in Parkanaur?"

Fizzle me feathers, what do you say? I mean Lily Grey Squirrel is a good friend of mine and I know, without a doubt, that she and her husband Norman don't want the red squirrels moving into Parkanaur, even if their ancestors were here first. Still, I'm a postcrow and in my job it's important to get on well with everyone.

"Of course, Terry, we all are. What a silly question. Didn't all the animals agree to your return at our last Parkanaur Residents' Meeting?" Squirm, squirm. Have you ever had to look someone in the eye and tell them something you know they want to hear but you know is not exactly the truth? Although I tried my best to sound convincing, Terry still seems unsure.

"It's Teresa. She's upset that no-one has been to say hello or ask how we're settling in and it's difficult for her anyway because neither Connor nor Geraldine wanted to leave our old home."

Rather than tackle the question as to why no-one had been to welcome them I enquire,

"Terry, if you don't mind me asking, why did you leave your old home?" Terry seems almost pleased to be given the opportunity to explain himself.

"I suppose it might seem a foolish thing for a squirrel to say, and I'm not sure if it applies to crows, but I wanted to return to my roots. For generations, stories have been passed down about what life was like for our ancestors here in Parkanaur Forest and especially about the kindness of the lady who lived in the Big House. I know the lady is no longer alive, but I just wanted to bring my family back to where I feel we belong."

Fizzle me feathers, this is worse than I suspected. Terry is talking about what Parkanaur was like years upon years ago. Can he really expect it to be the same today? Oh well, I suppose it's not for me to burst his bubble. Norman Grey Squirrel will be more than willing to do that for him! I think the best thing for me to do now is just to remove myself as tactfully as possible.

"Ah right, Terry, so you're returning to your roots. Lovely, well I have quite a large postbag this morning and time is getting on."

I swing my scarf round my neck, flap my wings and head down the Red Lane before Terry has a chance to respond. I'm not heartless you understand, and I know moving home can be difficult at the best of times, but why insist on moving to somewhere where you're not really wanted in the first place?

I've no post for Sandy Warren as Joseph and Madge Rabbit and their kittens are still away. Madge hasn't been at all well recently but I've heard she's much better and that they might be home soon. Next stop is Oak Drey, a letter for Lily Grey Squirrel. Perhaps I can persuade Lily to extend the paw of friendship to Teresa Red Squirrel, but then there's her husband, Norman. Norman Grey Squirrel hates red squirrels with a passion, all red squirrels! That looks like Lily's tail disappearing into the laurels.

"Lily! Lily, is that you? I've a letter for you."

Lily is a kind soul and is held in high regard by most of the residents in Parkanaur. It has to be said that many admire her for putting up with grumpy Norman, who seems to be permanently in a bad temper. As Lily pops out of the laurels she nearly knocks my cap off.

"Good morning, Charlie, and isn't it a fine morning?"

"It is indeed, Lily," I reply equally cheerfully as Lily's smile would brighten anyone's spirits, "here's your letter."

"Thanks, Charlie, looks like another bill. Normy gets upset when bills arrive so I get them addressed to me."

I feel I ought to ask about Norman, although if I'm honest it's more as a politeness to Lily, rather than any real interest I have in Norman's wellbeing.

"How's Norman today? I hope he's recovered from his cold."

"Actually, he's having a lie in this morning. He says he's still not feeling completely well. He believes those red squirrels probably brought germs with them when they moved into Parkanaur."

That's so typical of Norman, blaming his sniffles on the red squirrels and there's probably nothing wrong with him anyway.

The slightest little ache or pain and Norman takes to his drey for days. The injustice of blaming the red squirrels makes me suggest,

"I was thinking it would be nice if we arranged a little welcome party for Terry and Teresa and their young ones. I think they might be feeling a bit lonely."

"Oh I don't know, Charlie, you know how Normy feels about red squirrels. He probably would refuse to attend and even if he was persuaded to, well there might be angry words – or worse!"

No doubt about it, it's going to be difficult to persuade Norman to welcome Terry and Teresa Red Squirrel but the other animals will be watching his and Lily's behaviour before they make a move. At least I've made Lily aware of how Terry and Teresa are feeling, perhaps, I should leave the rest to her good nature. Oh fizzle me feathers there's the rain again.

"A day for the drey I think, Charlie! I've a letter for you if you could just wait a minute. It's for my sister, Marie."

As I shelter under the laurels waiting for Lily's letter, I think of what my Mother used to say, "Actions speak louder than words and silence speaks loudest of all." Let's just hope Lily can break the silence that is making Terry and Teresa feel so rejected.

Lily Grey Squirrel's Letter

Oak Drey

Parkanaur Forest

Dear Marie,

Norman, or Normy as I like to call him, is fast asleep so I can write this letter without worrying that he might read it and become upset.

A family of red squirrels has moved into the Deer Park in Parkanaur and Normy is furious. He hates them although he can't explain why he hates them. He says that you can't trust them, that everyone thinks they are so sweet but really they are sneaky little gits. When I suggest that we are all squirrels and are only different in colour, size and a few tufts in the ears, he explodes with anger. He is convinced that because we are greys and they are reds, we have been, and always will be, enemies. Marie, our Father taught us to respect all other creatures and I find it difficult to agree with Normy's attitude to our new residents but I do not wish to upset him.

Then there is the question of the little ones, they follow our example and what kind of example are we setting them? Just the other day I overheard Maisie telling Junior that he wasn't to play with Connor or Geraldine Red Squirrel - not even if they asked him to join in their games. When Connor asked her what was wrong with joining in their games, all Maisie could come up with was, "Father wouldn't like it".

It's all a worry to me and I would greatly value your advice.

Your loving sister,

Lily.

Marie Grey Squirrel's Reply

Bridge Drey

Leck Lane

Dearest Lily,

What a dilemma! I know how close you and Norman are and so I can understand that this difference of opinion is a great source of sadness to you. All I can say is what Father would have said to you, "Be true to yourself". If you believe that it is right to respect and befriend the red squirrels then that is what you should do. You will just have to be courageous and explain your point of view to Norman. I know it is not going to be easy, but you are a strong squirrel and you can do this.

Then there is Junior and Maisie to think about. Do you want them to grow up with this blind hatred of red squirrels? I do understand the problems such a stance will create for you. Norman is not a squirrel who likes to be disobeyed but he respects you and if he will listen to anyone on this matter, it is you, Lily. Do try to get to the bottom of why Norman hates them so much, only then will you have a chance of changing his mind about them. I will be thinking of you.

Your loving sister,
Marie.

3

Has Bert a Secret Plan?

You would think October would be a quiet month for a postcrow, wouldn't you? Well, not a bit of it, my postbag is bulging this morning. I really don't know how I'm going to manage when the Christmas rush starts. Never mind, a bit to go before we have to worry about that.

Admittedly, Marie-Claire Hedgehog, Percival and the piglets are settling down for the winter so no more letters there, just lots of snoring! Hibernation really only affects the hedgehogs and bats in Parkanaur so my postbag doesn't get that much lighter during the winter months. Gosh, but it's getting chilly these mornings, thank goodness for my Mother's scarf.

I suppose you are wondering how Bert and his plan to teach the humans a lesson is coming along. Well, to be honest, I'm not much wiser than you are. Hold on a minute, here's Rory Robin. He's one of Parkanaur's nosiest residents. If he doesn't know what's going on, no-one will.

"Caw, caw, caw! Rory, over here a minute." Rory makes a rapid landing on a nearby bush and covers his ears with his wings.

"For goodness' sake, Charlie, do you have to make such an awful racket? A simple chirp would suffice if you require my attention."

I feel I have to put him right.

"Actually, I don't do chirps, Rory. I'm a crow and nature has provided me with a rather effective caw and it would seem ungrateful of me not to use it. Anyway, now that I have your attention, have you heard anything about how Bert's plan is progressing?" At this Rory perks up. His beady eyes light up as he waves me closer with his wing and speaks to me in hushed tones.

"It's a secret, only the feathered residents of Parkanaur are to know about it. Bert's working on it as we speak."

Well, I'm very fond of Bert, as you know, but I'm not sure about this secret business. It seems no time at all since we all agreed to our Plan for All and said that we would try and help each other. Secrets don't seem to fit into that somehow. I don't like secrets, do you? Can't keep them for a start, before I know what's happening I've opened my beak when I shouldn't have and there's a row. I don't like rows either by the way.

Do humans have secrets? Do they cause problems for you too? It looks like I'm going to have to encourage Rory to spill the beans.

"Well, I'm a feathered resident, so it's okay for me to know about Bert's secret plan. What's he plotting?"

"I don't know, he says he can't tell anyone until he's ready to put it into action." Rory is clearly excited.

I have to confess I'm suspicious. It sounds to me as if Bert hasn't got a plan at all and by saying that it's secret he's trying to bluff everyone until he thinks of something. I've a letter for Kevin Otter who lives on the river bank upstream from the waterfall, so I think I will give Bert a little visit on my way past. We'll get to the bottom of this secret plan one way or another.

"Frank, frank."

Oh fizzle me feathers, that has to be Marjorie or Seamus, only the grey herons have that harsh, distinctive call. Yes, I'm right. Here he comes and I hope he's careful coming in to land. Have you ever seen anything like the wingspan of a grey heron?

"I suppose the fishing hasn't improved any, Seamus?"

"Indeed it has not, Charlie. I spent two hours absolutely motionless and got nothing, not a single fish. It's not on, you know, simply not on."

I look at Seamus' very long legs and wonder how grey herons do that. Just stand still for hours on end.

"Have you been speaking to Bert or heard what he's planning to do?"

"I haven't even seen him. I think he's hiding in that nest of his. All talk and no action, that Bert fellow, what do you think? Eh? Eh?"

So Bert isn't fooling Seamus either. As his friend, I really think I ought to put him straight. I'll just drop this letter off with Kevin Otter and then we'll get to the truth of this matter. Is there a plan or isn't there?

Sean Otter's

Dear Kevin,

I just wanted to let you know that Grainne and I are organising a slide party for next Saturday. We've made some excellent slides into the river near our holt and are inviting some friends along to try them out. The pups are welcome too as they are perfectly safe. It should be great fun.

Fishing has been good lately due to the heavy rain, especially down by Dead Hen's Dyke. Our only problem is that a family of mink has moved into the area and they seem to have rather large appetites, do you have any problems with these pests in Parkanaur?

One of the local humans is creating a pond and no doubt will be filling it with those fish daft humans seem to prefer, funny colours and fancy fins. Between the herons and the mink they'll probably last all of a week.

particular human is blessed with an

amount of common sense so perhaps he'll give

the fancy fish a miss. Anyway, Kevin, all the best and hope

to see you on Saturday.

Regards,

Sean.

Kevin Otter's Reply

Fisher Holt

River Torrent

Dear Sean,

Great to hear from you. Rita and I and the pups will be delighted to try out your slides next Saturday. Our slides are a bit the worse for wear and I suppose we really should think about replacing them.

We've had heavy rain too but the fishing has been really disappointing. The humans must be taking water from the river further upstream as the level is really low and we're not getting anything like the fish we should.

Strange you should mention mink, we had a real problem with them a few months ago. Then they began to kill the ducks on the pond and the forest rangers started to trap them. I haven't seen any for a couple of weeks now. It's those humans again, if they hadn't farmed the mink in the first place, they wouldn't have escaped into the wild and they wouldn't be pinching our fish.

Anyway, I'd better go. Regards to Grainne and the pups and see you Saturday.

Best wishes,

Kevin.

4

The Confession

This wind is a bother, I've nearly been blown off course twice! I can't help thinking about my friend, Bert Kingfisher. I know he was really rude to Marjorie Grey Heron, but that's not like him. He's hungry and he's worried. He's quite a serious sort of chap, worries about things too much if you ask me.

Bert isn't always an easy bird to track down, moves so fast you see. I know he likes to fish this stretch of the river, so I shall just perch here and wait patiently. I'm determined to speak to him beak to beak and ask him about this secret plan of his. Was that a flash of blue I just saw?

"Bert! Bert! Is that you, Bert? It's Charlie, I want a chat."

Oh fizzle me feathers, I don't think he heard me, he flies so fast. What I'd give to be able to fly like that! Oh thank goodness, he has heard me. He's heading back this way.

"Hello, Charlie, didn't see you there on my way downstream, had a bit of speed up."

Bert settles himself on a sturdy branch overhanging the river bank. He seems to be having difficulty looking me in the eye. I think the best way to deal with all of this is just to spit it out.

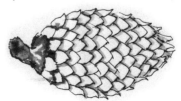

"Look, Bert, you know I'm your friend so you can tell me truthfully, have you got a secret plan or haven't you?" Oh fizzle me feathers, I've done it now, Bert is visibly squirming.

"Well, actually no, Charlie, I haven't. I'd like to have a secret plan. I'd like to know why the humans are taking our water. I'd like to have a plan to stop them that would teach them a lesson. But no, I don't have one. I can tell you the truth, but I've told others I have this secret plan and I can't admit to them now that I haven't."

Has this ever happened to you? It's certainly happened to me. I've made up a story and everyone thinks I'm wonderful and then I can't bear to tell them that it's not true. I don't think it was very clever of Bert to tell fibs and I don't think everyone even believes him, but he's my friend and I have to try and find a way to help him.

"Okay, Bert, not a good idea to say you had a plan when you hadn't, but let's see what we can do about this. First things first, we need to find out what the humans are doing with the river water. We need some spies. I shall speak to some of the other crows."

"Oh, Charlie, would you do that? I haven't been able to find out anything."

"Not a problem, I'll let you know as soon as I have some news. Let's just hope my friends can help."

It's nearly dusk so I'll head home to the rookery and see what the others have to say. I hope everyone is sympathetic. Nearly home now, gosh there's a lot of noise tonight. If Rory Robin thinks I'm loud I wonder what he would make of this lot settling down for the night? It's not going to be easy to get their attention!

"Caw, caw, caw! C'mon everyone, I need your help." Fizzle me feathers, they're all flapping down beside me to hear what I have to say. Oh well, here goes.

"Look, guys, I need your help, well actually, it's my friend, Bert Kingfisher, who needs your help."

"What's up, Charlie?" asks Barney, a very confident young crow, "Why does Bert need our help?"

I explain about the river water being so low, the lack of fish, Bert Kingfisher telling everyone how he had a secret plan to teach the humans a lesson when he had no plan at all and how foolish and embarrassed Bert is feeling now.

Then Christina, quite an elderly crow and known for her wisdom, hops forward.

"How does Bert Kingfisher know that it is the humans who are responsible for the lack of river water?"

"Well, when I think about it, he doesn't! Bert is just assuming that it's the humans who are diverting the water further upstream. None of us really knows if this is true or not."

Immediately another crow, Winston, who sees himself as a bit of a commander-in-chief, pipes up,

"Charlie, why don't we help you find out what's actually happening to the river water and then we can devise a plan. What I suggest is that we take to the air at first light in groups of five or six and examine different sections of the river upstream."

Well, this sounds like a very good idea to me and the rest of the crows agree. I know we have our differences, but it's at times like this that I'm glad to be part of a flock. You never feel alone and there's always help at wing in a crisis.

I had expected that, perhaps, some of the crows would have objected to my request for help, since the lack of river water doesn't really affect us very much and Bert's problem is rather of his own making. Not a bit of it, not a single caw raised in protest. We decide to get a good night's sleep to prepare ourselves for the task ahead.

. . . .

The wind didn't bother me one bit last night, I slept like a chick. But where is everyone? Lots of my fellow crows seem to be assembling in the car park. I wonder if someone chucked their chips out of their car last night, that always gets a crowd in the morning. I'll just fly down and see. Would you believe it? Winston and Barney Crow have used their beaks to draw a map of the river in the dust of the car park. They are sending off parties of five or six crows at a time. I'd better hurry up and volunteer for duty, but what about my post round?

Winston Crow is waving me over.

"Good morning, Charlie, everything's under control, areas have been identified and search crows are being dispatched at five minute intervals. We thought you would be too busy with your post round so we haven't counted you in. All crows are to report to me, in the Formal Garden, at twelve hundred hours."

Well fizzle me feathers, what do you think of that? On the one wing, I'm really pleased that Winston has taken the task of searching for the missing river water so seriously and is so well organised. On the other wing, I'm a bit miffed that I'm really not required at all. Anyway, I'd better get on with my post round.

Postcrows meet locally, shortly after daybreak, to sort the post and exchange letters. I'll just pop this letter of mine in my postbag before I meet the others. I don't really want anyone to see it, it's confidential. I want to be back to the Formal Garden in time to hear how the search parties got on. I hope my postbag is a light one this morning!

Charlie Crow's Letter

Charlie's Nest

Parkanaur Rookery

Dear Madam,

I know you will be somewhat surprised to receive this letter as I cannot imagine that you have too many pupils of the crow variety. However, I hope that will not mean you dismiss me as a hopeless case. For some time now I have had this desire to sing but I am aware that my voice is not entirely musical. The other day I was merely calling out to a fellow bird when he objected to the tone of my voice.

Improving my singing voice will be a challenge and I'm aware of that but I do hope you will help me. It's quite all right if you don't want me in a class with your other pupils because, to be honest, I'd rather keep this a private arrangement to begin with, as some of my fellow crows may not understand.

I do hope you will agree to help me.

Yours respectfully,

Charles Crow.

Josephine Song Thrush's Reply

Song Thrush Academy

The Garden

Drum Manor

Dear Mr Crow,

Thank you so much for your letter which I received from our postcrow, Mildred, this morning. You are quite correct in saying that we do not receive many requests from crows for tuition. In fact, I think I can quite safely say yours is the first. I am also in agreement with you that teaching a crow to sing would be a major challenge.

However, as a song thrush, it is my belief that the enjoyment of singing should be available to all. Not all my colleagues here at the academy agree with me on this. Several feel that if a pupil has no talent for singing that they should simply be dismissed and told the brutal truth that they are unmusical. I believe that if a bird, or an animal for that matter, wants to sing and enjoys singing, then we should help them if they ask for our assistance.

I must warn you though, Mr Crow, that the likelihood of your singing ever becoming truly musical, no matter how hard you study, is very slim indeed. Nevertheless, if you still want to try, please attend the Academy at four pm next Thursday afternoon.

Yours most sincerely,

Josephine Song Thrush. (Senior Tutor)

5

The Crows hold a Conference

Winston Crow is standing in the middle of the Formal Garden behaving as if he should be working for air traffic control. He's waving his wings about furiously and, as crows are coming in to land, Barney Crow is organising them and carrying out a debriefing. In other words, he's finding out what, if anything, they have learnt about the missing river water. There's lots of excitement and lots of noise. In fact, so much so, that it's attracting the attention of some of the other residents, including Terry and Teresa Red Squirrel, who are making their way up from the Deer Park. Winston addresses the crows in a loud voice.

"All search parties have returned safely and are accounted for so I am declaring this Crow Conference open. Barney, what have you to report?"

Barney Crow hops to the front of the assembled crowd of crows and turns to face the flock.

"Search Party Six reported that approximately three miles upstream from the waterfall the water is being diverted into what looks like a man-made pond."

So Bert Kingfisher was right after all, the humans are to blame. Winston Crow wants more information.

"Is this just for their amusement? Is there any evidence as to why these humans want a pond? Is it to decorate their garden or is there another reason?"

Barney Crow clearly doesn't know the answers to these questions and so he requests that a spokescrow from Search Party Six comes forward to address the Conference. A rather overfed, middle-aged crow, swaggers to the front of the flock and prepares to address the crowd. I recognise him as Clive. He roosts three trees down from me.

"We did fly over the area a number of times because, at first, it wasn't clear why the humans would want a pond there. It's in an ordinary field and certainly not part of any planned garden that we could see. Then we heard a familiar sound, a tractor engine. We watched and a farmer approached with a tractor and tanker. He got out and put a hose that was attached to the tanker into the pond and proceeded to suck up water. We didn't like the way he was looking at us and so we left." Throughout Clive's account, Winston Crow has been taking notes and immediately asks,

"What is this farmer called?"

"We don't know his name so we just referred to him as Farmer No-Name." Clive seems a bit taken aback by Winston's sharp tone. Winston Crow persists,

"Have you any idea what his purpose was in drawing the water into his tanker or why this Farmer No-Name wouldn't just have used his own water supply?"

"No, not really." Clive Crow is clearly becoming irked by this interrogation.

"Okay," says Winston Crow, "I'm opening this discussion up to the entire Conference. Can any crow throw light on this Farmer No-Name's behaviour?"

There's a lively debate amongst all the crows as to why this Farmer No-Name is drawing off the river water and using it to fill his tanker. Most farmers now have their own bore hole which means they can pump up whatever water they need and so they do not have to pay water charges for using the mains supply. Some farmers collect rain water. It would appear that Farmer No-Name may be too lazy to dig a bore hole and pump his own water or be bothered to collect rain water. He just finds it easier to steal the river water. Clive Crow wants to know why farmers need so much water anyway and Barney Crow tries to explain.

"Well the most likely reason he's taking water into that tanker is to wash out the manure, after all he's not allowed to spread manure on the fields after the end of October, not until spring comes again." Thinking of my river friends I ask,

"But what will happen if Farmer No-Name releases that dirty water back into the river, surely it will kill all the fish?"

"Yes it will," Winston Crow agrees, "the question is, how do we prevent him from using the river water?"

Christina Crow, who has obviously been pondering things, can't help wondering,

"What else does he do with all that water as well as wash out his tanker?"

Barney Crow, who is always keen to show off his knowledge, is happy to elaborate.

"Well, do you realise that a cow drinks five gallons of water a day and since farmers are no longer allowed to let their animals drink from the rivers, I guess he feels justified in taking the river water to them. He would have to use a different, clean tanker, for this purpose, of course. He probably also uses the water for washing his farmyard and outbuildings."

"Okay crows," Winston Crow is clearly anxious to stop the Conference going on too long, "so we know that it is this Farmer No-Name who is taking the river water and we think we know why he's taking it, what we need now is a plan to stop him taking any more of it."

"We'll have to find a way to sabotage his efforts, to make sure that he finds it more trouble to take the river water than it would be to dig a bore hole and pump his own water or to collect rain water."

"Well it took a genius to work that out, Barney," caws an exasperated Christina Crow, "but how are we going to make it more trouble?"

Clive Crow suggests that our entire flock should fly to this pond and flap around Farmer No-Name every time he takes his tanker to collect the river water. Christina Crow points out that this Farmer No-Name would probably just take out his shotgun and shoot us all. Being a crow of some intelligence, I put forward a more subtle plan.

"What if a small number of our best-beaked crows fly to this pond after dark, when Farmer No-Name has finished work for the day, and use our beaks to make drainage holes so the water seeps away." Although this is a cunning plan, Barney Crow has to point out,

"But Farmer No-Name will just repair it the next day."

"But the next night we make more holes and we keep making more holes every time he repairs the damage until he finally realises it would be easier to dig a bore hole or collect rain water!" Since no crow has a better idea, Winston Crow announces,

"It's agreed then. Operation No-Name will commence at eighteen hundred hours this evening, all those who wish to volunteer should report to the Formal Garden for beak inspection and the best six beaks will be selected for the first attack."

I can't wait to tell Bert Kingfisher all about Operation No-Name, he'll be really excited. I'll call with Terry and Teresa Red Squirrel first as I've yet more post for them. I hope it cheers them up as they both looked very lonely as they left the Formal Garden. I won't stay too long anywhere as I'd like to get back early and do some beak exercises before I present myself for inspection for duty this evening. I do hope I get selected for Operation No-Name's first attack. Do you think I stand a chance?

Ruby Red Squirrel's Letter

Ash Drey

Seskinore Forest

Dear Teresa,

How we all miss you! The girls met for a pine cone lunch today and everyone said that it just wasn't the same without you. Melvin is missing Connor, they were such good friends and he's really lost without him. Perhaps we will be able to visit you before the winter sets in. We could try hitching a lift with one of the forestry vehicles.

I do hope that everything is working out well for you. I know how much it means to Terry to be able to have Connor and Geraldine grow up in Parkanaur. I'm also aware, though, that sometimes things don't work out as we have planned. Still, the outcome of the Parkanaur Residents' Meeting did seem to be in favour of giving you a real chance of making a new life there.

We have had some very wet weather recently and have spent quite a bit of time in the drey, at least it gives me the opportunity to catch up with my letter writing.

Please try and write soon and let us know how you all are.

Missing you so much.

Your dear friend,

Ruby.

Teresa Red Squirrel's Reply

Lime Tree Drey

Deer Park

Parkanaur Forest

Dear Ruby,

Oh how I am missing you and my other friends in
Seskinore. I am so lonely since we moved to Parkanaur.
The residents here may have voted in favour of red
squirrels being allowed to come back to this forest, but we
have been made to feel anything but welcome. It is not
what the other animals are doing, it is what they are not
doing. Everyone keeps clear of us, no-one speaks to us,
except Charlie Crow who collects and delivers the post,
and no-one has been to visit us.

The humans have been kinder to us than our fellow
creatures. Alec, the forest ranger, has put up special
feeders for us and they are kept full of hazelnuts by the
local visitors to the forest.

If anything, this has made us even more unpopular.
Although it means we use less of the natural food supply,
instead of being pleased about this, the grey squirrels are

complaining of discrimination because they can't use the feeders. If they try to sit on the feeding platform their heavier weight causes it to collapse and drops them on the ground!

Terry is miserable and feeling guilty about bringing us here, so do please try to organise a visit. It would cheer us all up.

Your loving friend,

Teresa.

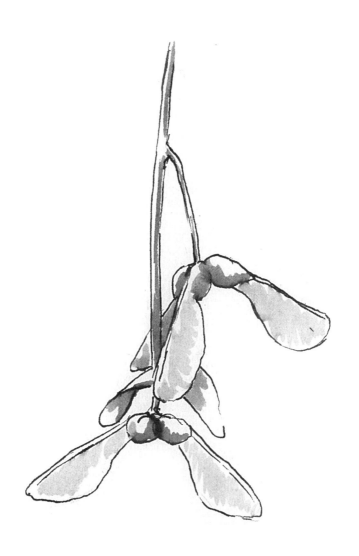

6

Will Mavis Help?

"What's all this about Operation No-Name then?"

"Fizzle me feathers, Rory, who told you about Operation No-Name?"

"Barney Crow is telling everyone that only six, select crows, are flying a special mission tonight and he's going to be one of them!" That's so typical of Barney Crow, all beak and no brains. Some secret mission this is going to be if Barney Crow is blabbing to the entire forest. I really don't want to get into this with Rory Robin.

"Have you seen Terry or Teresa Red Squirrel at all? I really think they would welcome a visit."

"Do you think I have taken leave of my senses, Charlie? If I'm seen making friends with Terry Red Squirrel that Norman Grey Squirrel will make my life not worth living. You forget Norman and I are neighbours round by the pond."

"Didn't think you'd be so easily intimidated, Rory, I thought you were your own robin. Did you not agree, with the rest of the residents, to welcome the red squirrels back to Parkanaur Forest?"

"Who was it, Charlie, said at the time that actions speak louder than words? Have you seen one animal or bird visit

Lime Tree Drey or offer a welcome paw or wing full of acorns or beech nuts? I don't think so and guess what, I'm not going to be the first! What's more, I'm not perching around here to be lectured to by you. I'll see you later."

Oh fizzle me feathers, this is dreadful. Why did all the animals and birds agree to welcome the red squirrels back if they weren't going to honour their words? Norman certainly made his feelings known, but when it came to the Plan for All even he didn't object to having the red squirrels back, providing there was only a small number of them and they were restricted to the Deer Park. Terry and Teresa Red Squirrel and their family are the only ones to have returned so far and they are living in the Deer Park. They are sticking to what was agreed, so why is no-one befriending them?

I do have my beak exercises to do before six o'clock, but on my way to tell Bert Kingfisher the news about Operation No-Name I think I'll call in with Mavis Wood Mouse at the Dry Stone Arch. Mavis is such a kind hearted soul and a great cook. Maybe she would visit Teresa Red Squirrel and take her some of her Nutty Delights! I'll just call with her now.

Flippity flap and down I glide. I wonder if it's too early to call on Mavis, she may not be up yet. It's late afternoon but she may still be snoozing. Oh, it's nearly dark so I'll give her a try.

"Mavis, are you up yet?"

"Is that you, Charlie? What brings you calling at this time?"

Poor Mavis, she looks so sleepy and is yawning for all she's worth.

"I'm so sorry, Mavis, I know it's very early for you, but I was hoping you could do me a favour."

"Of course, Charlie. I always try to help when I can, you know that."

"It's Terry and Teresa Red Squirrel, no-one is making any effort to make them feel welcome here in Parkanaur Forest, well none of the residents anyway. I was wondering if you would call with Teresa and take her some of your Nutty Delights. What on earth do you put in them anyway to make them taste so good?" With that Mavis has a fit of the giggles. Mavis often has a fit of the giggles.

"Okay, Charlie. I'll bake some Nutty Delights this evening and pay Teresa Red Squirrel a visit soon. I have been meaning to visit but with the little ones, it's not easy to fit everything in."

"Thanks, Mavis. You really are a gem and I know it will mean a lot to both Terry and Teresa Red Squirrel. See you later."

Right, my visit to Bert Kingfisher is going to have to be mighty brief if I'm going get these beak exercises done and make it back to the Formal Garden in time for beak inspection.

"Charlie! Charlie! Just a minute, I've a letter here you could take for me, if you would be so kind."

"Gosh, Mavis, I was nearly away, good thing you squeaked when you did."

The river's certainly still very low. Just look at it at the big bend between the old chestnut and the broken Deodar Cedar. It should be swirling round that corner after all the rain we've had. Although it's nearly dark Bert is still searching for fish.

"Charlie, is that you? Any word?"

"Hello, Bert, yes, in fact that's the reason I'm here. I haven't got long but you'll be pleased to hear what's planned for this evening."

Mavis Wood Mouse's Letter

Nest-in-the-Burrow

Dry Stone Arch

Parkanaur Forest

Dear Georgina,

Sorry I haven't replied to your letter sooner but you know what a dreadful correspondent I am. I'm kept so busy with the family and, of course, we've all been feasting furiously to make sure we have plenty of weight on for the winter. Feasting is one of my favourite pastimes, hee, hee, as you well know.

I've been thinking I should visit Parkanaur's new residents, Terry and Teresa Red Squirrel and their family. We did all agree to them moving into the Deer Park but none of us has exactly made them feel welcome. I thought, perhaps, I would bake some of my Nester Nibbler Specials or Nutty Delights and take Stephen with me. His daymares are not as frequent as they were and he's growing in confidence again but that Rupert Fox has a lot to answer for. Still, at least our son escaped his grasp.

Harry sends his kind regards and he and I both hope you and Fred and the family can come and see us soon.

We expect to be here until at least the end of October but Harry has been talking about trying to move into the kitchen of the Big House, just for the coldest months of winter – do you think we are wise?

Look forward to hearing from you.

All my love,

Mavis.

Georgina Wood Mouse's Reply

Tree Trunk Bottom

The Limes

Dear Mavis,

What a nice surprise to receive your letter this morning.
I was delighted to hear that Stephen is feeling a bit
better and I know our Mary will be too, I do believe she's
still quite sweet on him.

I'm a bit concerned about your decision to befriend
Terry and Teresa Red Squirrel. It seems to me that
if none of the other Parkanaur residents are making
any effort to welcome them – should you? You may
upset some of the other residents, particularly the grey
squirrels, and I could just imagine that Norman Grey
Squirrel being quite nasty. Anyway, you must decide
what's best, dear, but do be careful.

Now, about Harry's idea of moving into the kitchen
of the Big House, well, Fred would advise against it.
Apparently his second cousin, Sam Wood Mouse, came
to a very unpleasant end in that same kitchen last
winter.

It seems the humans set mousetraps everywhere but
Sam was confident he knew where they all were and

could avoid them. Then one night he stepped in some awful glue stuff they had put out and his exhausted little corpse was seen being taken out by the humans the next morning.

It's Fred's belief that a little cold weather and lack of food, whilst difficult, may be the lesser of the two evils. However, if Harry decides you should move, be sure to let me know so I can address my letters to you correctly.

Take care my dear.

Very best wishes,

Georgina.

7

Operation No-Name

Fizzle me feathers, I've been selected as one of the six beaks to attack Farmer No-Name's pond banks. Must have been those beak exercises that did the trick. Thank goodness it's a night time operation so my post round is no problem. Winston Crow is in charge of operations and we are just being lined up for take-off.

"Now, remember you guys," Winston Crow seems sincerely concerned for our safety, "if you get into trouble, get out and get out fast! Good luck everyone."

This is the most excitement there's been for ages. I do hope we can successfully sabotage Farmer No-Name's pond and then Bert Kingfisher and all the river birds will have plenty of fish again. We've just passed the waterfall, we're following the river upstream, it won't take us long to get to our destination.

"Everyone, maintain beak silence," whispers Barney Crow who is our leader on this mission, "we're nearing our target."

My heart is pounding. I do hope my beak is up to the task. Just as we're approaching the pond we can see where Farmer No-Name has made a thick dam across the river and is diverting the water on to his land where he's obviously dug out the soil to make room for a pond. Now that I'm here I can see that it is the dam we need to attack. Attacking the banks of the pond won't work as our beaks couldn't make big enough holes

for the water to seep away quickly. Destroying the dam would not only frustrate Farmer No-Name more than letting the water seep out of his pond but, more importantly, it would restore the river water for Bert and his friends. Unfortunately, this thought has obviously not dawned on our leader.

"Right guys," whispers Barney Crow, "get to work on the pond banks, spread yourselves out round the edges of the pond and get drilling with those beaks."

"But Barney," I try to protest, "surely…"

"Quiet, Charlie!" Barney glares at me but still speaks in a whisper, "What did I say about maintaining silence? Now get drilling!"

"It's just that…" I don't finish my sentence because Barney shoots me a look that would wither a rhinoceros. Perhaps I'm wrong, but I reckon even if we can drill enough holes in the pond banks for the water to seep out, it will happen so slowly that the river water that is being diverted by the dam will just keep filling the pond up again. All this won't help send the water back down the river. What we really need to do is destroy that dam.

"Help! Help!" cries one of our group, "Barney's beak is stuck in the clay!"

I look round and sure enough, Barney Crow is stuck fast by his beak in the clay of the pond bank! He's squirming about but because his beak's caught he can't say a word! I'm tempted to point out that it must be a first for Barney not to be giving orders but I rise above this uncrowlike thought. Instead, I try to think of a way to release him.

"Gulp some water," I whisper loudly, "and try to squirt it around his beak so the clay becomes slimy rather than sticky."

"Okay, we've done that, Charlie, what do we do next?"

"Keep squirting the water around his beak and a couple of you grab him from behind and pull."

Slurrrrrrr-p! Thank goodness, Barney Crow's beak has come out and it's in one piece. He's not amused though.

"You really didn't need to pull me that hard!" he shouts angrily.

All this fuss has really not helped us in our mission and just as I thought, any water our drill holes have released has been replaced already. I'm aware that Barney Crow is unlikely, after his ordeal, to be any more sympathetic to what I have to say but I feel I must try.

"Barney, I really think it's the dam we need to be drilling rather than the pond banks." Fizzle me feathers, I get it said before Barney has a chance to interrupt me! He must still be suffering from shock!

"Who put you in charge?" His beak is quivering with rage. I think he lost his dignity getting his beak stuck in the clay and now my challenging his instructions is just too much. Why is he letting his pride get in the way of his common sense? Barney's an intelligent crow and if he would just think about this he would realise I'm right. Are humans as daft as this? Do they let their pride get in the way of their common sense? I'm sure they don't.

"I'm just trying to be helpful, Barney."

"Well don't."

The other four crows in our group of sharp beaks all start
arguing about whether or not I'm right and whether we should
try to drill holes in the dam or whether Barney's right and we
should continue to drill holes in the pond banks. The debate
is getting more heated and our whispers are becoming louder
and louder until I realise we're shouting and then,

"Bang! Bang!" It's Farmer No-Name and he's firing at us
with his shotgun.

"Quick! Quick!" Barney Crow yells at us, "Remember what
Winston said, let's get out of here, everyone into the air now!"

As we disappear into the distance, Farmer No-Name lets
off another couple of rounds but thankfully none of us gets
hurt. No-one utters a caw on the flight home. Approaching
the Formal Garden we can see that Winston has organised
our fellow rooks to hold their white faces upwards to mark the
central path as a landing strip for us. As the sixth crow lands,
Winston Crow hops forward.

"Well, crows, how did it go? Did you succeed in destroying
the target?"

This is embarrassing. It's up to Barney Crow to reply since
he is our leader, but is he really going to tell the entire flock
that we failed because we squabbled so loudly we alerted
Farmer No-Name, I don't think so. We wait as Barney Crow
starts to explain.

"Not exactly, once we arrived at the pond we realised things
weren't as straightforward as we had at first thought. I pointed
out that as well as drilling holes in the pond banks, to ensure
the success of the mission, we would also have to destroy the
dam."

Well fizzle me feathers! He's stolen my plan! What a downright nasty, sneaky, underwing thing to do. Of course, if I say anything it will look as if I'm trying to take the credit for his idea. He's still talking.

"We made a start on the pond banks. As you can probably see from the clay on my beak, I worked particularly hard. Unfortunately, before we could tackle the dam, Farmer No-Name opened fire on us with his shotgun." As soon as he says this, there is a gasp from the assembled crowd of crows. Winston Crow realises the mission has failed.

"Do you think you will be able to make another attack on the dam tomorrow evening?"

Suddenly, I realise that Barney Crow is not the crow he appears. He talks big but I can see in his eyes that he's afraid. The business of his beak being caught in the clay and being shot at by Farmer No-Name has completely undermined what limited courage he ever had. Before Barney Crow can open his beak to make an excuse, I find myself speaking,

"Actually, Winston Crow, we discussed this tonight," - well if Barney Crow can make things up then so can I - "and we agreed that in order to drill through the dam we would require longer length beaks. Farmer No-Name has packed the area beneath a tree trunk across the river with branches and mud. We would also require specialist equipment to remove the displaced earth."

"Good grief!" Winston Crow exclaims, clearly shocked, "Is that it then? Do we have to admit defeat?"

"No," I reply, feeling somewhat pleased with myself, "I don't believe we do, I think I know where we can find just the help we need."

"Excellent! Where do you propose to find this help?"

"Well, Seamus and Marjorie Grey Heron have very long and sharp beaks and they could drill right through the lower section of the dam and Malachy Mallard's beak is perfect for hoovering up and removing the earth we displace. Since this mission will directly benefit them, I'm sure they'll help." I'm sitting, feeling very satisfied with myself, when suddenly Barney Crow shrieks,

"But they're not crows. This is a crow mission!"

Can you believe this? This is the crow that is too scared to go back to finish the work himself but he's going to object to Seamus, Marjorie and Malachy helping out. I think I know how to handle this one.

"You're right, Barney Crow, probably best if you lead the attack on the dam again tomorrow night." Almost at once Barney has a complete change of heart.

"Oh no, Charlie, I don't think that would be right, they're your friends and I had thought, perhaps, I should stay and help Winston Crow with ground control. On reflection, you're quite right to bring in specialist help, no reason why we shouldn't work together with our fellow feathered friends on this mission."

It's agreed by everyone that in the morning I should talk to Seamus and Marjorie Grey Heron and Malachy Mallard regarding another attack on the dam. I'm to be leader of this new mission as Barney Crow is going to help co-ordinate matters on the ground. What an evening! Tomorrow could be even more exciting. I've a letter for Seamus Grey Heron so I might just call in on my way home. I wonder what he'll think of our plan?

Hughie Grey Heron's Letter

Hughie's Nest

The Heronry

Drumcairne Forest

Dear Seamus,

I know it is some time since I have written but my duties as Secretary of the "Help the Heron Society" are taking up more and more of my time. I have to confess our own heronry here at Drumcairne Forest is, naturally, uppermost in my priorities, but branches are springing up everywhere and so my workload is increasing all the time. I was wondering if you would have any interest in spearheading a branch in your own area.

Hazel and I have been enjoying some special treats thanks to Mrs Frazer. Mrs Frazer owns the large bungalow I was telling you about – with the fish pond – the well-stocked fish pond! Well, it was well-stocked until last Tuesday when Mrs Frazer went for her weekly shop and Hazel and I helped ourselves to her fish. Oh, they were so plump and scrumptious! Needless to say, Mrs Frazer was not best pleased. She has restocked her pond but, sadly, has covered it with fine mesh, so no more treats I'm afraid.

Never mind, at least there's been plenty of rain and the river is fairly deep, and if those wretched fishermen would leave them alone, we should have a decent supply of fish. I do hate to see them on the river but I can't help feeling they're kindred spirits. They're one of the very few creatures who can match us for patience when it comes to fishing!

We look forward to hearing from you and catching up on your news.

Kind regards,
Hughie.

Seamus Grey Heron's Reply

Heron Nest No 2

Bend-beyond-the-Waterfall

Parkanaur Forest

Dear Hughie,

Great to hear from you at last, thought you'd lost the power of your beak! Bit jealous to hear about Mrs Frazer's fish, you are a jammy old soul.

We're having a terrible time of it here in Parkanaur. The river is barely trickling over the waterfall in spite of all the rain we've had. I can see the weight dropping off my poor Marjorie.

Bert Kingfisher reckons it's the humans who are responsible – some kindred spirits then. Eh? Eh? Anyway, Charlie's got the crows involved and they're investigating further to find out what's really happening. I hope we get it sorted soon or poor Marjorie will be feathers and bone.

I'll let you know what happens but feel free to write to us in the meantime.

Yours,

Seamus.

P.S. I'll ask around to see if there's any interest in starting a branch of the "Help the Heron Society" in this area. Judging by recent events, we could do with all the help we can get.

8

The Fight

"Seamus! Seamus! It's me, Charlie. Did you get your letter? I left it last night but you were asleep." Seamus Grey Heron flaps down beside me and nearly blows me over with the breeze from his enormous wings. He is quickly followed by Marjorie.

"Are you sure that letter's not for me, Charlie? I'm expecting news of a happy event from my cousin."

"Patience, dear, patience," Seamus smiles at Marjorie.

I assure Marjorie that as soon as her letter arrives I will deliver it as a matter of urgency. In the meantime I need a favour. I explain all about Operation No-Name and how we'll really need long, sharp beaks to drill through the dam on the river.

"Gosh, Charlie, this is great news, isn't it, Marjorie? Great news. Eh? Eh?"

"It is indeed, and, of course, we would be more than willing to help. What else are friends for?"

"Oh I don't know about you dear, I mean from what Charlie has told us about this Farmer No-Name, this could be dangerous work, dangerous work. I'm not sure that you should take part. She's delicate you see, Charlie, delicate."

"Stop fussing, dear, of course I'm taking part. I'm not as delicate as you think and two beaks are better than one."

Oh fizzle me feathers, I hope I'm not going to start a matrimonial row. Seamus is very protective of Marjorie but as I stare up at her vast size, in bird terms, delicate is not the word that immediately comes to mind.

"Well, Marjorie, if you're sure, you and Seamus would certainly make a good team."

"Oh yes, that's true, Marjorie and I certainly make a good team. Okay, dear, if you're sure, if you're sure, we can work together on this. Eh? Eh?"

"Of course I'm sure, dear, we can do some practice drilling into the river bank this morning, just to get our technique polished up a bit." I leave Seamus and Marjorie discussing beak movements regarding the best method to break through the dam quickly and easily.

I've a letter for Rory Robin so I head towards the pond where there's a good chance I'll find Malachy Mallard as well. There's Rory near the litter bin.

"What's happening? Do you need any help? Robins have sharp beaks you know."

"Who told you we needed help, oh, I've a letter for you here somewhere."

"There's not much happens in this forest that I don't know about. I hear Barney Crow made a bit of a prat of himself last night. I also hear you need more sharp beaks and, as you can see, mine is severely sharp!" I ignore the comment about Barney Crow because, whilst I agree with Rory, I still feel a certain loyalty to a fellow crow.

"Your beak might be sharp enough to poke worms out of the

ground, Rory, but I hardly think it's strong enough to drill through a dam."

"And how would you know, Charlie Crow? Have you drilled through many dams?"

"No, but I do know how thick this dam is and how strong your beak is!"

"I could work my way through in stages – or I could widen the beak holes made by Seamus and Marjorie Grey Heron so the water would break through more quickly."

"Who told you Seamus and Marjorie Grey Heron would be drilling holes?" There may be very little Rory Robin doesn't know but I'm not sure how useful or otherwise he would be in helping to drill the dam. He's fearless so he wouldn't panic if there was trouble, on the other wing, he's not exactly what you would call a team player.

"Let me think about it, Rory, and I'll get back to you. I do appreciate your offer of help." Of course, I know that Rory hasn't offered to help out of the goodness of his heart. He's just so nosey and loves to be in the thick of things. Still, he might be useful, so it's best to keep our options open.

Now, I need to find Malachy Mallard. Where can that duck be? Are those his orange feet I see on the island in the middle of the pond? Perhaps, he's at home after all.

"Malachy! Malachy Mallard! Is that you over there?"

"Hi there, Charlie, hold on and I'll swim over to you."

Malachy reaches me in an instant and, yet again, I start explaining about Operation No-Name and why we need his help.

Malachy's a decent sort and agrees at once to come along. I start to explain that we are all meeting in the Formal Garden before dusk for our pre-mission briefing when Lily Grey Squirrel comes flying through the trees at top speed.

"Oh, Charlie, come quickly, they're going to kill each other!"

"Calm down, Lily, who's going to kill whom?"

"Normy and Terry Red Squirrel, they're fighting in the Deer Park." Rory Robin just can't help himself.

"Do they think they've turned into fallow deer and are joining in the rut?"

"That's really not funny, Rory," says Lily. She is clearly in a very distressed state and although every other creature in the forest finds her husband, Norman, a pompous pain, for some reason that is beyond us all, Lily loves him.

"Look, Lily, don't panic, we'll all come now and put a stop to this."

"Oh thank you, Charlie, you're a true friend."

Fizzle me feathers, I know Norman Grey Squirrel and Terry Red Squirrel have their differences but I thought they were going to live and let live. I wonder what provoked this fight?

As we are all flapping our way up the Red Lane to the Deer Park we can see two angry squirrels fighting furiously. Poor Lily Grey Squirrel is following us as fast as she can. There are times when wings do have the advantage over paws. Rory Robin is clearly enjoying this spectacle but Malachy and I immediately do our best to break it up. Malachy gets in between the fighting squirrels, flapping and quacking for all he's worth. I try to appeal to their common sense.

"I don't know what this is all about but stop it now!

We can sort it out without resorting to pawsicuffs!" Lily Grey Squirrel and Teresa Red Squirrel, who are now standing side by side, plead in unison,

"Please stop! Please stop!"

The fight is now attracting a lot of attention. As well as me, Rory Robin, Malachy Mallard and the squirrels' wives looking on, the fallow deer are making their way towards the commotion, with Owen Fallow Deer leading the herd. No-one messes with Owen Fallow Deer, especially in the rutting season! When we spot him trotting over the brow of the hill, the assembled group, including Norman Grey Squirrel and Terry Red Squirrel, scarper to the other side of the Deer Park gates. As we all flap and scamper to the ground, at a safe distance from Owen Fallow Deer, I ask the question on everyone's mind,

"What started this? What's this all about?"

"I told you there'd be trouble if you let those reds back into Parkanaur."

"No, Norman, actually you didn't. When we held our Residents' Meeting, you agreed with the rest of us, that a small number of red squirrels could return to the Deer Park. Terry and Teresa Red Squirrel and their family are the only red squirrels who have returned so far and they have made their drey in the Deer Park."

"That might be correct, Charlie, but I found that Connor Red Squirrel on the Red Lane eating our beech nuts!"

Terry Red Squirrel is clearly furious.

"He's only young, he doesn't understand and you didn't have to frighten the life out of him, you big bully. No-one's going to treat a young'un of mine like that."

Oh fizzle me feathers, they're going to start fighting again! I'll have to do something.

"Okay! Okay! Remember we are the adults here. Norman Grey Squirrel, you have to realise that Connor Red Squirrel is very young and has just moved here, he hasn't learnt the rules yet. Terry Red Squirrel, to avoid any recurrence of this bother, perhaps, you should sit down with Connor and Geraldine and explain the situation to them."

"Yeah, sure, Charlie. Tell me, how would you like to explain to these innocent, little, native squirrels, that they have to stay within the boundaries of the Deer Park whilst those grey, foreigner squirrels can have the run of the forest?"

Fizzle me feathers, this isn't easy. All I'm trying to do is keep the peace. Lily Grey Squirrel, a squirrel of integrity and reason, puts a paw on her husband's shoulder which is starting to quiver with rage, and steps forward.

"This is difficult for all of us. None of us are responsible for the actions of our ancestors. We do not consider ourselves foreigners as we were born in this forest. We feel we made a compromise in agreeing to red squirrels returning to the Deer Park. Mistakes have been made on both sides. You should have explained the terms of your return to your young but Normy should not have intimidated a little squirrel in such a manner. What I suggest is that we put this entire incident behind us and start again."

There is an awkward silence but eventually there is a rather begrudging nodding of heads. Thinking that it would be a good idea to seal the deal I suggest,

"C'mon, chaps, why not shake paws on it?"

"There's no need to go that far," grunts Norman Grey Squirrel and turns to walk away. Lily gives me a look which suggests that, perhaps, I was asking just a little bit too much. She follows her husband.

"What did I tell you, Charlie. All this let's all love one another just doesn't work in practice."

"Oh shut up, Rory! Here, read your letter."

"Well I was just saying ……."

"Well don't!"

I have to be honest with you, I'm disappointed with this turn of events, aren't you? I mean, I didn't expect Norman Grey Squirrel and Terry Red Squirrel to become best buddies overnight but to be actually fighting each other, this is going to make things more difficult than ever. The last thing we need is for Terry, Teresa and their family to become even more isolated. Oh well, I've still a few deliveries to make so I'd better get going. That looks like Joseph Rabbit outside Sandy Warren and he's got a letter in his paw. I do hope his wife, Madge, is feeling better. She's had a terrible time.

Gerry Robin's Letter

Gerry's Nest

Beech Tree

Church Lane

Dear Rory,

I have been meaning to write but you know what's it like, trying to find food is taking more and more of my time. It's true that Mrs Higglebottom, she's the sexton's wife, they live just next door to the church, does put out food for the birds but sometimes she forgets us robins.

You know what the humans are like now, all these fancy feeders where they can watch the blue tits and other show-offs swing upside down and perform acrobatic feats – not a boring bird table in sight! I was so hungry last winter that I nearly broke a leg attempting to hold on to one of those wire peanut feeders. I mean we robins simply aren't built for that sort of contraption. Luckily, Mrs H saw me and from then on she put some breadcrumbs on the window sill – when she remembered!

I was delighted to hear that you told that grumpy, old Norman Grey Squirrel a few home truths at your Residents' Meeting. I suppose the red squirrels will have moved into Parkanaur by now. I wonder how that will work out, do write soon and let me know.

Best wishes,

Gerry.

Rory Robin's Reply

Rory's Nest

The Pond

Parkanaur Forest

Dear Gerry,

The red squirrels, one family on a trial basis, have moved into Parkanaur and what do you think? There's been a fight already! Can you believe it? Well you probably can because you know what a grump Norman Grey Squirrel is. Apparently, he found young Connor Red Squirrel eating beech nuts on the Red Lane. I have to confess none of the residents here have made much of an effort to make the red squirrels feel welcome. Well, I mean why should we? They wanted to come here, we didn't ask them. I suppose we were waiting to see how the grey squirrels would react. Guess we've got our answer!

No-one was hurt in the fight. Malachy Mallard and Charlie Crow intervened before they really got going. Rather a pity as I do like a good squabble. Let's face it, we robins are involved in them all the time! Besides, squirrels aren't exactly our best friends, are they?

You mentioned the lack of bird tables in your letter but when did you last see a bird table that wasn't raided by those pesky squirrels? Red or grey, they seem to have a sixth sense when it comes to the location of a well-stocked bird table.

Must go now, but I'll keep in touch and let you know how things progress with our new residents.

Bye for now,

Rory.

9

Wing Command Attacks!

Fizzle me feathers, secret mission my tail feathers. It's not even dusk yet and would you look at the number of animals and birds assembled in the Formal Garden. One family's missing though, Terry and Teresa Red Squirrel have obviously taken things to heart. The fallow deer were born in the Deer Park so they know nothing only captivity, but Terry and Teresa and their family have known a very different life. Giving up your freedom is a high price to pay for returning to your roots.

Rather than being annoyed at the lack of secrecy which has led to this large assembled crowd, Winston and Barney Crow are strutting about in a very self-important manner, clipboards under wings and issuing orders like no crow's business.

"Kingfisher Squadron, line up for take-off!"

Fizzle me feathers, I didn't even know Bert and his mates were taking part in this mission and I'm supposed to be leading it!

"Wing Commander Charlie Crow – to the gazebo for a final briefing!"

As I hop over to the gazebo I can see Barney Crow organising the other squadrons for take-off. Malachy Mallard has rounded up a few fellow ducks to help with the earth removal and Rory Robin has obviously decided that territorial disputes are not as important as being involved in Operation No-Name. He and a number of robins are also getting into formation. I note he has exchanged his usual sunglasses for a sturdy pair of goggles. Seamus and Marjorie are being directed to the rear of the other birds and are looking rather bewildered. Winston Crow hops into the gazebo beside me and is all business.

"Okay, Charlie, it's over to you now. You know what you have to do. Get in, destroy the target and get out. We'll count you off, remember the ducks, and especially the herons, will take longer to get airborne. You need to get your formation right once everyone is in the air. Good luck." I take off first and before I know it Bert Kingfisher is right beside me.

"Bert, keep your distance, I know you're speedy but reserve your energy for drilling the dam."

"Will do, Charlie, sorry, just so keen to get going. I really want to teach this Farmer No-Name a lesson."

"That's understandable, Bert, but we need to work as a team. We need to maintain a steady speed until everyone is in the air and in position." The rest of Wing Command is forming up without any problems. Everyone knows we need to maintain beak silence and that the flight path follows the river upstream until we reach the target.

Discipline is good this time, beak silence is being maintained without further orders and there she is – our target! Just as I'd predicted, the pond has filled up again. This time we're going to hit the dam itself. As we loosen the earth Malachy Mallard and the ducks are going to lift it and transport it in their beaks. They're going to deposit the earth at the entrance to Farmer

No-Name's pond to block it off. Then when we destroy the dam made by Farmer No-Name the river water will follow its natural path downstream.

Seamus and Marjorie Grey Heron start drilling the lower section of the dam, slow and steady. At the same time the crows swoop, as agreed, to the left and right flanks, attacking in short, sharp bursts. As earth starts to come free, Malachy Mallard and the other ducks begin to hoover it up and start filling up the entrance to the pond. Bert and the kingfishers are hovering in mid- air. Bert whispers,

"What do you want us to do, Charlie?"

"I want you and the robins to attack the dam from the other side. Use your sharp beaks to pick out any pebbles or small stones that are helping to hold the dam together."

"No probs, Charlie, we're on our way." Bert Kingfisher starts diving into the wall of the dam like something possessed. I'm worried he's going to damage his beak.

"Take it easy, Bert, you'll need that beak for fishing when we get this river flowing again." Everyone is trying really hard but the crows keep getting their beaks stuck and have to stop and help each other release them. Then Seamus Grey Heron whispers,

"Charlie, this is going to take forever, the mud is really thick and we're getting tired already, so are Bert and his friends, none of us have had much to eat these past few days." Fizzle me feathers, what's to be done? We can't return a second night and admit we've failed. Barney Crow would be unbearable and our friends really need some fish soon. We'll retreat and hold an emergency meeting.

"Right, chaps, follow me back downstream, we need to review the situation in an area of safety." The squadrons obey my order without question and follow me to a field close by.

"Okay," I'm keeping my voice low just in case there are any humans around, "we need to review our strategy – any ideas?"

"It's the thickness of the mud in the dam, Charlie," Seamus explains, "even Marjorie and I are having trouble breaking through."

"Say Seamus does break through, it's still going to take lots of work before the dam gives way." This comment is made by Samantha Crow who, as well as having an extremely sharp beak, is a very intelligent young crow. She continues,

"What we really need is a battering ram, something much stronger than our beaks."

"When I was on the other side of the dam, I saw a large piece of timber near the riverbank. Follow me and I'll show you," says Bert Kingfisher. We are all infected by Bert's enthusiasm and everyone is about to take to the air when Samantha Crow points out,

"Even if this piece of timber is exactly what we need, we'll never be able to lift it, much less batter the dam with it!"

Oh fizzle me feathers. I decide we should go and inspect this piece of timber anyway so I remind everyone that we still need to maintain beak silence in the air and keep in formation. Bert Kingfisher will fly slightly ahead of me, to my right wing, to show us the way.

"It's massive, Bert," I whisper, "we'd need a lot of help to get it into the river."

"Even if we got it into the river – would we be able to get enough power behind it to batter through the dam? Eh? Eh?" asks Seamus Grey Heron. Just as Seamus is scratching his head with that enormous wing of his, Samantha Crow pipes up again,

"Right, I've got a plan. We're going to need a lot of help but it's well past dusk and most residents will be up and about so that shouldn't be a problem. We need to do three things. Firstly, we need to get this pond of Farmer No-Name's blocked off so the pressure of the water coming downstream is all being forced towards the dam. Secondly, we need to move this massive piece of timber further upstream so when it hits the dam it does so with the full force of the gushing river. Finally, we need to make a weakened target area on the dam for the crew on the timber to aim for." Everyone seems somewhat overwhelmed by Samantha's plan but it makes good sense to me and so I start issuing orders.

"Bert, you're the fastest. Head downstream immediately, stop at every home and tell them we need their help. Explain how important it is that they make no noise and no fuss and give them our exact location. I'll issue them with further orders when they get here."

"Already on my way, Charlie."

"Right, the rest of you start gathering soil, twigs, pine cones – anything you can find and pile it up at the entrance to the pond."

"Charlie, it's no good," says a flustered Malachy, "We've been trying to block the entrance to the pond but as soon as we lay down some soil, the water just washes it away."

"Okay, so what we'll do is we'll start to gather everything on the bank beside the entrance to the pond. The others can help when they arrive with larger pieces of material. Then we'll dump a huge dollop of everything we can find into the entrance, all at the same time, and plug that pond once and for all!"

As the squadrons disperse and start gathering from the forest floor, the first of the back-up auxillary forces arrive. They're led by Kevin and Grainne Otter and their pups, followed by Cyril and Cynthia Fox with their son Alexander – who has had the nerve to give me a letter for the post! Then Patrick Badger is being helped along by his wife, Jennifer, who is waving their cubs on ahead of them. Joseph Rabbit is there, as is Mavis Wood Mouse and her brood, as well as Norman and Lily Grey Squirrel. What a turn out!! It's amazing how helpful everyone is in a crisis. Mind you, I expect that tomorrow they'll all be bickering as usual!

I explain Samantha Crow's plan and give everyone their orders. The otters and badgers and foxes are going to try to move the timber further up the riverbank to give it more time to build up speed. I'm a little concerned by the noise the beaks are making trying to drill through the mud in the dam. Bert Kingfisher is attacking pebbles like some sort of demented demon. Terry Red Squirrel appears out of nowhere, on his own, with some old rope.

"Charlie! Charlie! I found this old rope. The forest rangers must have dropped it. If we could tie a piece of rope to either side of the timber before we launch it into the river and pull it back so we catapulted it, imagine how much more force we could create!"

"Excellent, all squirrels on rope duty now – we need your teeth and agility."

Norman Grey Squirrel looks at me and I know what he's going to say but then his wife, Lily, whispers in his untufty ear. Whatever objections Norman Grey Squirrel was going to make about Terry Red Squirrel being out of the Deer Park, or about having to work with him, have been shelved for the time being. The squirrels gnaw the rope in two and attach it to either side of the piece of timber. Meanwhile everyone else has collected a huge pile of forest rubbish and placed it beside the entrance to the pond. I explain that we need a few big pieces of broken branches to act as a framework for the soil, leaves, pine cones and whatever else they've collected. We will drop them in first and then everything else will stick to them, rather than be washed away. Immediately, the larger animals scurry off to find some big bits of branch. There has to be precision in the execution of this operation. As Wing Commander this is up to me.

"Right, on the count of one everyone will get ready, on the count of two the badgers, otters and foxes will drop the broken branches into the water at the entrance to the pond and on three everyone else will drop or push whatever they can in on top of the broken branches. Is everyone ready?"

"Yes!!"

"One.....Two.....Three!" It's working! It's working! Can you believe it? We've plugged the pond!!

"Pilots on board and prepare to launch timber!" Everyone scurries back upstream to where the timber is.

I've appointed Norman Grey Squirrel and Terry Red Squirrel as pilots to steer the timber towards the target area of the dam. I hope they can continue to work together as I need the strength of the badgers, otters and foxes to pull back the ropes restraining the timber. Everyone wants in on the act and is picking up a bit of rope wherever they can. With the pond cut off, the force of water is building against the dam. I have to take charge again quickly.

"Are you ready? After three let her go – one…two…three…"

As the timber hurtles towards the dam we can see that Norman Grey Squirrel and Terry Red Squirrel are struggling to keep it on target but they manage to do it and just before it hits the dam they leap off to either side of the river. Thank goodness squirrels are so good at leaping – at least that's one thing Norman Grey Squirrel and Terry Red Squirrel have in common! As the timber hits the weakened area of the dam it breaks through, a little water pours through at first but then, more and more as the wall crumbles. In the excitement of the moment we all start to cheer.

"Bang! Bang!" It's Farmer No-Name and his shotgun. Everyone runs and flies as fast as they can, in all directions. I'm afraid Wing Command discipline has disintegrated as everyone is making their way home as fast as possible. Still, no need for a debriefing tonight as everyone will be talking about what happened. I would have liked to have waited around to see Farmer No-Name's face but I think it's safer just to imagine it – don't you?

Alexander Fox's Letter

Denvale Earth

Parkanaur Forest

Hi Lola,

Thanks for keeping in touch and sorry I wasn't able to make it on Tuesday night, hope you didn't wait around too long for me. Mumsy and Pops absolutely insisted I did some hunting with them over by the Scout Hut. Of course, I would have much rather spent the evening with you.

There's a bit of a buzz in Parkanaur, something to do with the river being low. As long as I can get a drink, which I can, I'm not that bothered. Charlie and the rest of the crows seem to be getting very excited about it all – sad lives they have, that's all I can say.

I've spotted a few rabbits, plump and a bit on the slow side, here in Parkanaur. What about meeting me on Saturday night, usual time, usual place and we could have ourselves a little sport and supper?

See you then,

Lexi.

Lola Fox's Reply

East Earth

Heather Bank

Alexander,

I waited for ages on Saturday night, by the blackberry patch just north of the Five Sycamores. This is the third time in as many weeks that you haven't turned up after you have arranged to meet. I was so looking forward to a little raw rabbit for supper but I was also looking forward to seeing you again.

I've heard you were involved with the destruction of the dam and that you have been impressing that young vixen, from above the waterfall in Parkanaur, with tales of your daring antics. She obviously doesn't know you as well as I do.

This note is just to let you know you needn't twitch your whiskers at me anymore, I've had enough. I really don't care if we never chase a chicken or race after a rabbit together again – ever!

Good-bye,

Lola.

10

Danger and Destruction

Everyone was in such high spirits after our successful mission against Farmer No-Name. Sadly, our celebrations have been overshadowed by the events of the past few days. Strangers have invaded our forest and are destroying it. They're using chain-saws to cut down all the laurels and rhododendrons. Can you imagine the amount of homeless there are going to be amongst my feathered friends? Trying to deliver the post is a total nightmare. They're even cutting down trees. Lily and Norman Grey Squirrel lost Oak Drey and have had to relocate to a Scots Pine close by. Here's Rory Robin, he might have some news.

"Hello, Rory. Have you had a chance to find out what's going on?"

"Vandalism! That's what's going on, Charlie. I don't believe our forest has ever been in such a mess. It's not Alec or any of the other forest rangers. It's some strangers that have been brought in. It seems they're trying to prevent the spread of diseases that are killing the trees."

"Oh fizzle me feathers, that's typical, save the trees but never mind about the wildlife."

"Wise up, Charlie, trees have always been more important to the humans than wildlife." Rory Robin pushes his dark glasses on to his forehead. I know, it's October, but Rory always wears his shades. He beckons me closer and says in a confidential tone,

"Did you know traps have been spotted behind the Thuja tree?"

"Oh not again, has anyone told the grey squirrels?"

"Not sure, Charlie, I mean would you want to be the one to tell Norman Grey Squirrel?"

"No, but I'll certainly have a word with Lily Grey Squirrel, thanks for telling me."

"I'm going to be out and about today, Charlie, so I'll let you know if I spot any traps elsewhere in the forest."

"Thanks, Rory, talk to you soon."

Oh fizzle me feathers, on top of losing their home and having to relocate, I now have to bring this news to Lily and Norman Grey Squirrel. I don't know about you, but when I've something tough to do, I just like to get on and do it. I'll head to Scots Pine Drey now and warn Norman and Lily about the traps.

Flippity flap, flippity flap, almost there. Good grief, there seems to be a real commotion on the path near Scots Pine Drey. Lily and Norman Grey Squirrel are both on the path, young Maisie Grey Squirrel is there too and they're talking to Malachy Mallard, some of the other ducks and Bert Kingfisher. Lily seems very concerned about something. She's calling me over.

"Oh Charlie, have you seen Junior on your post round? He's

missing and we've just heard that there are traps in the forest again. I'm so worried."

"Now, now, Lily," I try to be reassuring, "you know Junior is a sensible squirrel and you've warned him about traps. He's probably just checking on some acorns he's buried for the winter."

"Do you think so, Charlie? Do you really think so?"

Norman Grey Squirrel, who for some reason is looking guilty, suggests,

"We could check the Red Lane, he might be there."

Lily, who knows her Normy extremely well, is immediately suspicious.

"Why would we check the Red Lane, Normy? Why do you think Junior might be on the Red Lane?"

"Well, I might just have said something about needing to check that young Connor Red Squirrel was staying in the Deer Park, and not out on the Red Lane again, eating our beech nuts."

"Norman, why do you do such things? Isn't it bad enough that you hate red squirrels with such a passion without teaching Junior and Maisie to hate them too?"

Lily must be angry. She hardly ever calls her husband Norman. What's worrying me is that if Junior Grey Squirrel has gone to the Red Lane, that's very close to the Thuja tree where Rory Robin saw the traps. I don't want to worry Lily any more than she already is, so I simply offer to fly over and check if there's any sign of Junior Grey Squirrel on the Red Lane.

"Oh would you, Charlie? As the crow flies is always the

quickest way, thank you so much."

As I approach the Red Lane I see something I'm not expecting. Connor Red Squirrel is indeed on the Red Lane again, and Junior Grey Squirrel is there too, but unlike their fathers, they're not fighting – they're playing!

Although I think this is great, for their sakes, I need to do something before Norman Grey Squirrel arrives on the scene.

"Caw, caw, caw! Connor Red Squirrel, what's the meaning of you being out of the Deer Park again? Get home immediately!" Connor's face grows even more red than usual.

"Junior Grey Squirrel, your Mother is worried sick about you. Get back to Scots Pine Drey this instant!"

Well fizzle me feathers, I must sound quite authoritative for a crow because both youngsters scamper off without any protest whatsoever. I suppose they're both aware if their fathers had caught them they would have been in even more trouble! Talking of fathers, here comes Norman Grey Squirrel, followed by Lily. Lily throws her paws around Junior which makes him squirm with embarrassment. My dear Mother would have done exactly the same. I used to squirm too when she publicly threw her wings around me – I didn't mind in private though. Isn't that strange? Oh gosh, Normy doesn't look happy.

"Junior, son, was that young Connor Red Squirrel I just saw scampering over the Deer Park fence?"

"Yes, father."

"The nerve of the brat. I wonder if his Father spoke to him at all about not straying outside the Deer Park. Glad to see you sent him packing son, well done!"

"Yes, father, but it does seem a bit unfair that…."

"Unfair! Unfair! I'll tell you what's unfair, those wretched feeding boxes in the Deer Park, that's what's unfair. The humans fill them up with hazlenuts, if you don't mind, and if we try to use the feeders we fall on our backsides! Those red squirrels come back into our forest and are treated like royalty– now, that's unfair! They need to be taught their place."

Poor Junior, he realises, wisely, that this is not the time to try to reason with his Father and so turns and follows his Mum down the Red Lane. Norman Grey Squirrel doesn't follow them, saying that he needs to chat to some friends. Friends?!! Since when did Norman Grey Squirrel have friends?

As I reach the bottom of the Red Lane I turn left and fly up the river to the waterfall. Bert Kingfisher has flown ahead of me and is perched on his usual branch. The water is gushing over the stones of the waterfall and the river is surging downstream, almost breaking its banks at the bend by the chestnut tree. I've never seen a happier looking kingfisher.

"Gosh, Bert, the river is living up to its name today!"

"Torrent by name and torrent by nature, Charlie, this is what our river should be like after all that rain. Thank you so much."

"You're welcome, Bert, delighted we got things sorted. Pity we couldn't get the squirrels sorted too."

"You've done your best, Charlie. No-one could try harder than you to keep the peace in this forest."

"Oh well, I suppose I'd better get on with my post round. There's another problem needs sorting. All these homes destroyed by the destruction of the undergrowth. I've no idea what to do with some of these letters, the addresses simply don't exist anymore. At least I'll be able to deliver this one to Malachy Mallard, his home's still safe."

Abraham Mallard's Letter

Abraham's Abode

Eskragh Lough

Dear Malachy,

What a week we've had. First of all we had everyone in a flap because mink had been seen on the west bank of the lake. It turned out it was only old Mr Jameson's cat! Still, I know we need to be cautious.

Then, much more serious, was the drama surrounding Samuel Swan. As you know, we have quite a few fishermen use our lake. We don't mind that much because, generally speaking, they are quite thoughtful. They don't drop litter and they throw us their crusts from their sandwiches. Friday's events have changed everything, although to be honest, the fishermen were as upset as we were.

Sammy Swan was out on the lake, fishing as usual, when a fish hook got caught in his neck. There was a tremendous commotion, not just Sammy and the other swans but the fishermen as well. In fact we believe it was the fishermen who sent for the rescue humans.

They had huge nets but in the end one of them got close enough to throw his coat around Sammy and capture him. The rescue humans got the fish hook out and Sammy is fine but we are all a little more wary of the fishermen now.

Hope things aren't as frantic with you.

Kind regards,

Abe.

Malachy Mallard's Reply

Malachy's Retreat

Island-on-the-Pond

Parkanaur Forest

Dear Abe,

You only think things have been frantic with you. You won't believe what's been going on here this week. Some farmer upstream had built a dam and was taking the river water for himself. We taught him a lesson he won't forget. I played a vital role in a major operation to destroy the dam and return the river water to its rightful path. It was all tremendously exciting. In fact, life seems a little dull now it's all over. Phyllis is relieved things are back to normal but I enjoyed the action.

We had a bit of bother with mink here in Parkanaur, a few of our fraternity were actually killed by them so do remain vigilant. We were fortunate that the forest rangers set some traps and got rid of the blighters. It's peaceful and safe here now if you fancy flying over for a chat. I could give you a guided tour upstream and show you where we destroyed the dam.

Hope to hear from you soon.

Yours,

Malachy.

11

Another Crisis!

Fizzle me feathers, what is that racket? It sounds like it's coming from the Deer Park. I've my postbag ready so I shall just get my cap and scarf on and fly in that direction first. Oh my goodness, there's a bunch of grey squirrels with placards on the Deer Park gates. Norman Grey Squirrel is leading the chanting.

"Weaker in wisdom,
Weaker in weight.
Reds are rubbish,
Greys are great.
Run, reds, run
Accept your fate!"

Teresa Red Squirrel has Connor and Geraldine by the paws and all three look terrified. Terry Red Squirrel, tail flicking, is heading towards the gang of grey squirrels. I do admire his courage.

"What's your problem, Norman Grey Squirrel?" asks a defiant Terry Red Squirrel, "We're in the Deer Park and we're not eating your food. What possible reason have you for terrifying a mother and innocent little ones?"

"Nothin' innocent about that Connor Red Squirrel.

That son of yours has been out on the Red Lane twice eating our beech nuts. We want you out of here, you're not welcome. Do you hear?"

At this the gang of grey squirrels start chanting again. Teresa Red Squirrel has ushered Connor and Geraldine back into the safety of Lime Tree Drey but Terry Red Squirrel is trying to shout something back at Norman Grey Squirrel. I can't hear what it is as the chanting of the grey squirrels is drowning out Terry's words. I don't like this. It's bullying of the worst kind but I know Norman and the others won't listen to me. But here's someone he will listen to. Lily Grey Squirrel doesn't even notice me as she races past.

"Normy! Normy! Junior has gone missing again, he'd left the drey when I woke up and he's still not back. Normy, what are you doing here? Who are all these squirrels?"

"Perhaps you'd be better paid taking care of your own family instead of terrorising mine!" shouts Terry Red Squirrel from the other side of the Deer Park gates.

Norman Grey Squirrel jumps off the gates with raised paws but Lily yells out,

"Normy! We need to look for Junior now! Rory Robin says there are traps all over the forest."

Although Norman's behaviour totally disgusts me, Lily is my friend, and I hate to see this normally bright and cheerful squirrel so distressed. I offer to round up as many residents as I can muster to search the forest for Junior Grey Squirrel. We know we have a little time because the lady in the white van always comes in the late afternoon. The traps don't kill the squirrels, they capture them alive. Then this lady comes and takes them away in her van. We've heard she takes them to the university to test for squirrelpox, but she never brings them back.

The forest is full of birds and animals looking for Junior Grey Squirrel. No bird or animal likes to be trapped so everyone is helping with the search. Hours have passed and he still hasn't been found. Norman Grey Squirrel has had to take Lily back to Scots Pine Drey, she's exhausted and so upset. I'm making one last sweep through the Sitka Spruce near where we hold our meetings but still no luck. Who's this coming scampering through the trees? Oh no, it's Connor Red Squirrel and he's out of the Deer Park again! If Norman Grey Squirrel hears about this, in the mood he's in, I don't know what will happen.

"Charlie! Charlie! Come quickly, I've found him, I've found Junior Grey Squirrel!"

"Oh fizzle me feathers, are you sure, Connor?"

"Yes, yes, he's over here, follow me." As I follow Connor Red Squirrel through the Sitka Spruce my heart is pounding. Will it really be Junior Grey Squirrel and will he be okay? Then I hear it, a weak, scared cry.

"I'm over here, please help me, I'm over here."

Sure enough, Connor Red Squirrel takes me straight to the trap and there is Junior Grey Squirrel, frightened but otherwise fine. Connor Red Squirrel and I work together with paw and beak to try to free him. If we'd more time we could get help but the lady with the white van might come at any moment, it's getting late now. Then, out of nowhere, Terry and Teresa Red Squirrel appear.

"Can we help, Charlie?" asks Terry Red Squirrel, "I know

106

we shouldn't be out of the Deer Park but we realised our son, Connor, had gone to look for Junior Grey Squirrel, and despite his father's behaviour, we didn't want to see any harm come to the young squirrel."

"You certainly can help. We're having real problems with this contraption of a trap."

We all work at the trap and I'm not quite sure how we manage it but, suddenly, Junior Grey Squirrel is free. He's weak and a bit wobbly so Terry, Teresa and Connor Red Squirrel all support him. Terry Red Squirrel is concerned to get him to a place of safety as soon as possible.

"Charlie, Lime Tree Drey isn't far. We'll take Junior there for a rest and some hazelnuts if you want to fly over to Scots Pine Drey and let his parents know that he's safe."

"I'm on my way!"

"Lily! Norman! We've found him! We've found him!"

There's such excitement at Scots Pine Drey. Lily is weeping and Norman, grumpy Norman, is doing a jig with pure delight. I explain how it was Connor Red Squirrel who found their son and that Terry and Teresa Red Squirrel helped to free him and have taken him back to the safety of Lime Tree Drey. Norman, Lily and little Maisie Grey Squirrel all scurry off to the Deer Park to fetch Junior and take him home. As they do so, Rory Robin arrives on a branch beside me.

"So it was the red squirrels who rescued him?"

"Yes, Rory, it was indeed."

"So do you think Norman Grey Squirrel will thank them or ask them what they were doing out of the Deer Park?"

"Oh fizzle me feathers, Rory, even Norman Grey Squirrel has

to make the reds welcome now."

Rory drops his shades from his forehead.

"You wanna bet?"

The End

Charlie's Nest

Parkanaur Rookery

Dear Reader,

I have popped a little section at the back of this book to get you thinking, talking and even doing - hope it works!!

I've called it: Questions, Discussion Topics and Activities. Rory Robin didn't think that was very original but when I invited him to come up with something better - guess what? He didn't!

I'm always delighted to hear from my readers so why not visit my website at:

www.postcrow.com or my facebook page at:

www.facebook.com/fizzlemefeathers where you will find my contact details.

Hope you liked the book -do let me know if you did.

I must fly as I'm late for my post round.

Bye for now,

Charlie.

Chapter 1 – Rain but no Water!

Questions

1. What are Charlie Crow's two favourite trees in the forest?

2. Why is Charlie Crow surprised that the river is not higher?

3. Why do you think Bert Kingfisher perched on a branch overhanging the waterfall?

4. What is it about Bert Kingfisher that Charlie Crow envies?

5. Which part of a kingfisher is made especially for fishing?

6. Who does Bert Kingfisher blame for taking the river water?

7. Give two reasons why you think Seamus and Marjorie Grey Heron found it easy to wade up the river.

8. What kind act has Marjorie Grey Heron seen the humans do that makes her defend them?

9. Why is Bert Kingfisher not convinced by what Marjorie Grey Heron has to say about the humans?

10. What does Bert Kingfisher decide he is going to do?

Discussion Topics

Do you think Marjorie Grey Heron was right to defend the humans?

Discuss why birds differ when it comes to size, colour, beaks, legs and feet/claws.

Activity

Create your own bird. Paint a picture or make a model of it and describe the special features you have given it and their purpose, e.g. webbed feet so that it can swim easily.

Chapter 2 - New Residents

Questions

1. Why are the forest rangers trapping the grey squirrels?

2. Why did the returning red squirrels accept the restriction of living only within the boundaries of the Deer Park?

3. Charlie Crow is a postcrow. What does he do?

4. Charlie Crow is a rook. Name three other varieties of the crow family.

5. Why is Teresa Red Squirrel upset?

6. Why did Terry Red Squirrel want to move his family to Parkanaur Forest?

7. What is the word for a squirrel's home?

8. Why is Charlie Crow annoyed with Norman Grey Squirrel?

9. Why does Charlie Crow feel it is so important that Norman and Lily Grey Squirrel are seen to welcome Terry and Teresa Red Squirrel and their family?

10. What is the weather like at the end of the second chapter?

Discussion Topics

Terry and Teresa Red Squirrel and their family have not
been made feel welcome in Parkanaur Forest.
How important is it that we make newcomers in our
community welcome and how might we do this?

Grey squirrels, urban foxes and badgers are not popular
with everyone.
In each case discuss why some people do not like them,
what action, if any, they take against them, and whether
or not you feel their actions are justified.

Activity

Design either a poster in defence of grey squirrels or one
making a case for them to be killed.

Chapter 3 – Has Bert a Secret Plan?

Questions

1. Why does Charlie Crow's postbag not get much lighter during the winter months?

2. Who is described as one of Parkanaur's nosiest residents?

3. Why does Charlie Crow find it necessary to tell Rory Robin that he doesn't do "chirps"?

4. When Charlie Crow asks Rory Robin about Bert Kingfisher's plan, what three things about Rory Robin's response suggest he is excited?

5. Why is Rory Robin reluctant to discuss Bert Kingfisher's plan?

6. Why is Charlie Crow suspicious that Bert Kingfisher may not have a plan at all?

7. Why is Charlie Crow a little concerned when he sees Seamus Grey Heron coming in to land close to him?

8. Has the fishing improved any for Seamus Grey Heron?

9. What is it about the behaviour of grey herons that puzzles Charlie Crow?

10. Does Seamus Grey Heron think Bert Kingfisher has a plan?

Discussion Topics

Charlie Crow does not like secrets.
What kinds of things do people try to keep secret and why
do secrets often cause trouble?

Bert Kingfisher is convinced humans have taken the
river water and by doing so have caused him hardship-
as well as the kingfishers and grey herons, what other
birds and wildlife might depend on the river water?

Activity

In this chapter three bird calls are mentioned.
Make your own recording or listen to one of bird calls.
Make a chart which gives the bird's name and what its
call sounds like.
E.g. Robin – Tic, tic, tic

Chapter 4 – The Confession

Questions

1. How does Charlie Crow explain Bert Kingfisher's rudeness to Marjorie Grey Heron?

2. Why do you think Bert Kingfisher had trouble looking Charlie Crow in the eye?

3. What does Bert Kingfisher confess to Charlie Crow?

4. Why does Charlie Crow feel that he has to find a way to help Bert Kingfisher?

5. What does Charlie Crow think is the first thing they need to find out?

6. What word is used to describe a group of rooks' nests?

7. Who does Charlie Crow ask for help?

8. What important question does Christina Crow ask?

9. What does Winston Crow suggest they do?

10. Why did Winston Crow not include Charlie Crow in the search?

Discussion Topics

Why do you think Bert Kingfisher pretended he had a secret plan when he didn't?
Discuss what problems can arise from misleading others.

Charlie Crow tried to help Bert Kingfisher although he hadn't told him the truth.
Do you think he was right to do so?
Should we always support our friends?

Activity

Charlie Crow is a good friend to Bert Kingfisher.
Design your own Friendship Charter listing the top ten qualities you think a friend should have.

Chapter 5 – The Crows hold a Conference

Questions

1. What important discovery was made by Search Party Six?

2. What had Farmer No-Name been observed doing?

3. Why do most farmers collect rain water or dig bore holes?

4. Why did Farmer No-Name steal the river water instead?

5. What three uses might Farmer No-Name have had for the river water?

6. Which use particularly worried Charlie Crow and why?

7. What does Barney Crow say they will have to do?

8. What plan does Charlie Crow suggest?

9. How does Charlie Crow defend his plan against Barney Crow's criticism?

10. What name is given to this plan, when is it to take place and who is to take part?

Discussion Topics

The risk of river pollution is mentioned in this chapter.
Discuss causes of pollution and how they could be
avoided.

Water is one of the world's most important resources.
Discuss ways in which it could be better conserved and
distributed.

Activity

Draw up a water conservation and anti-pollution policy
for your home, school or local community.

Chapter 6 – Will Mavis Help?

Questions

1. Why is Charlie Crow shocked that Rory Robin knows about Operation No-Name?

2. Why does Rory Robin say that he can't be seen making friends with Terry and Teresa Red Squirrel?

3. Do you think Rory Robin is surprised that Terry and Teresa Red Squirrel have not been made feel welcome in Parkanaur Forest?

4. Why does Charlie Crow feel it is unfair of the animals not to welcome Terry and Teresa Red Squirrel?

5. Why does Charlie Crow decide to call in with Mavis Wood Mouse?

6. Mavis Wood Mouse sleeps during the day. What word is used to describe animals that sleep during the day and come out at night?

7. Do you believe Mavis Wood Mouse that she had intended to visit Teresa Red Squirrel? Give your reasons.

8. Why is Charlie Crow's visit to Bert Kingfisher "going to have to be mighty brief"?

9. Why is it unusual for Bert Kingfisher to still be searching for fish when it is nearly dark?

10. Why do you think Bert Kingfisher will be pleased with Charlie Crow's news?

Discussion Topics

Rory Robin obviously feels intimidated by Norman Grey Squirrel.
Discuss ways in which neighbours, friends, family or peer groups can intimidate individuals and how the individual can overcome this pressure.

Mavis Wood Mouse agrees to visit Teresa Red Squirrel.
How important is it that we make time to think of others and act kindly towards them?
Discuss acts of kindness that make a difference and cost nothing.

Activity

Carry out one kind act that will make a difference to someone you know.

Chapter 7 – Operation No-Name

Questions

1. Who is in charge of Operation No-Name and what advice does he give the crows involved?

2. As they approach the pond what does Charlie Crow see?

3. What does Charlie Crow think the crows need to do and why?

4. What misfortune happens to Barney Crow, the mission leader, and how does Charlie Crow suggest the other crows help him?

5. What do the crows argue about?

6. What happens as a result of their argument?

7. When Barney Crow gives his report of events why is Charlie Crow shocked?

8. Why does Charlie Crow suggest they need Seamus and Marjorie Grey Heron and Malachy Mallard on the next mission?

9. Why does Barney Crow object?

10. Why does Barney Crow change his mind?

Discussion Topics

Was Barney Crow a good leader of the first mission?
What qualities do you think make a good leader?

Pride prevented Barney Crow from listening to Charlie
Crow during the mission.
Can you think of instances where people have let their
pride get in the way of achieving a better result?

Activity

Choose a real person or someone who lived in the past or
a character from a book whose leadership you admire.
Write about this person explaining why you chose them
and what it is about them that you think makes them a
good leader.

Chapter 8 – The Fight

Questions

1. Why is Seamus Grey Heron reluctant for his wife, Marjorie, to help with Operation No-Name?

2. What amuses Charlie Crow about Seamus Grey Heron's protective attitude towards his wife, Marjorie?

3. Why does Charlie Crow ignore Rory Robin's comment about Barney Crow "making a bit of a prat of himself last night"?

4. As the crow that is to lead the second mission, Charlie sees reasons for and against having Rory Robin involved. What are these?

5. What started the fight between Norman Grey Squirrel and Terry Red Squirrel?

6. What does Charlie Crow suggest to prevent further trouble?

7. Why does Terry Red Squirrel find it difficult to carry out what Charlie Crow suggests?

8. How does Lily Grey Squirrel react to what Terry Red Squirrel has to say?

9. What suggests that Norman Grey Squirrel is still not happy about things?

10. Why does Rory Robin seem quite pleased?

Discussion Topics

Norman Grey Squirrel and Terry Red Squirrel find it difficult to see each other's point of view.
Discuss how important and difficult it sometimes is to see something from someone else's point of view.

Connor Red Squirrel should not have been eating beech nuts on the Red Lane but did that give Norman Grey Squirrel the right to frighten him?
Discuss the importance of having right on your side and whether or not it makes it acceptable for you to behave in ways which you usually wouldn't.

Activity

Agree on five things you and your friends argue about.
Hold a secret ballot in which each person votes for one of these as the most important cause of arguments.
Repeat the exercise with only boys and only girls voting.
Do the results differ?
Suggest ways to resolve arguments surrounding all five causes.

Chapter 9 – Wing Command Attacks!

Questions

1. Why does Charlie Crow think it is harder for Terry and Teresa Red Squirrel and their family to be confined to the Deer Park than it is for the fallow deer?

2. As well as crows what other types of bird are taking part in this second mission?

3. Where does Charlie Crow receive his final briefing from Winston Crow and what are his orders?

4. What prediction of Charlie Crow's has come true?

5. Why does Seamus Grey Heron say that it's going to take forever to break through the dam?

6. What do they decide to use to help them break through the dam?

7. What is Samantha Crow's plan?

8. How exactly do they block the entrance to the pond?

9. Who are the pilots on the timber battering ram and what do the other animals do?

10. How is Farmer No-Name alerted to their activities?

Discussion Topics

The successful attack on the dam required all the birds
and animals to work together.
Discuss times when you have worked as part of a team or
observed others doing so.
What was achieved and could one member of the team
have done it on his or her own?

When things weren't working out well, Charlie Crow
decided that they should review the situation and come
up with a different strategy.
Was this the correct decision?
In what other circumstances can you imagine it being a
good idea to review your strategy?

Activity

Make a model of the area of the river, the pond and the
dam to illustrate how the water from the river was being
diverted by Farmer No-Name.

Chapter 10 – Danger and Destruction

Questions

1. What is being done in the forest in an attempt to prevent the spread of diseases which could kill trees?

2. What effect has this had on the wildlife?

3. What has been spotted behind the Thuja tree?

4. Why will this discovery be a double blow to Norman and Lily Grey Squirrel?

5. What has happened to Junior Grey Squirrel?

6. Why is Lily Grey Squirrel angry with her husband, Norman?

7. What does Charlie Crow find happening on the Red Lane?

8. Why does Connor Red Squirrel's face grow even more red than usual?

9. Why does Junior Grey Squirrel decide it is not the time to reason with his Father?

10. Why is Charlie Crow surprised when Norman Grey Squirrel says that he needs to chat to some friends?

Discussion Topics

Rory Robin clearly believes that trees have always been more important to humans than wildlife.
Do you agree with him?

Lily Grey Squirrel is annoyed with her husband, Norman, because she believes he is teaching Junior and Maisie to hate red squirrels as much as he does. Do you think parents and other adults influence how you feel towards other people?

Activity

Find out what organisations protect trees and what ones protect animals.
Do any protect both?

Chapter 11 – Another Crisis!

Questions

1. Charlie Crow hears a racket in the Deer Park. What is going on?

2. Who is terrified?

3. How does Norman Grey Squirrel justify what he and the other grey squirrels are doing?

4. What news does Lily Grey Squirrel bring?

5. Why does Lily Grey Squirrel yell at Norman Grey Squirrel?

6. Who is the lady in the white van and why does she collect the grey squirrels?

7. Why is Charlie Crow concerned when he sees Connor Red Squirrel scampering through the trees?

8. Who rescues Junior Grey Squirrel?

9. Why is Junior Grey Squirrel taken to Lime Tree Drey?

10. Is Rory Robin convinced that after all that has happened, Norman Grey Squirrel will now make red squirrels welcome in Parkanaur Forest?

Discussion Topics

Charlie Crow describes the behaviour of Norman Grey Squirrel and the other grey squirrels as "bullying of the worst kind".

Why is it that people also behave differently in a mob?

How can you avoid becoming part of a mob?

In countries all over the world there are groups of people who don't like each other because of race, religion, culture or historical differences.

Research examples of this worldwide.

Can you think of any ways in which we can make future generations more tolerant?

Do you think Norman Grey Squirrel's attitude to red squirrels will change?

What changes people's attitudes to each other?

Activity

Draw a comic strip or cartoon with an anti-bullying message.